THE SHADOWS OF TERROR

Book One of the Patterns Series

Russell F. Moran

The Shadows of Terror

ACKNOWLEDGEMENTS

As always, I thank my wife, Lynda Moran, for being my first editor, critic, and contributor of great ideas and suggestions. She makes the art of storytelling fun. After my first draft of any novel, Lynda digs in and helps me bring the story to life. She's also kind enough to laugh at my jokes.

I also thank my friend and editor, John White for his eagle-eye reading of the book.

Brenda Judy, my "editor-in-chief" from Florida, gave me guidance and story insight that only a real pro can provide. You can find Brenda at Publishersplanet.com.

I also thank my readers, the people who are really what a novel is all about. I write for them.

AUTHOR'S NOTE

This book is fiction, and any similarity to actual people is a pure coincidence. But you may find parts of the story in your morning paper, because the book starts with real events, and then let's those events surround the characters.

Please note – A Cast of Characters for this book is found after the end. Nothing can be more frustrating, especially if you've been away from a book for a few days, to find a character on pate 205 who you first met on page five, and you can't remember who the guy is.

THE SHADOWS OF TERROR

CHAPTER ONE

We all knew it was coming.

We'd seen it before, yet we chose to believe it wasn't happening.

But now our world has changed.

A morning habit for most people has become a national custom. You turn on the TV, catch up on the weather, and see the latest news of the day or what happened overnight. Some have a TV in their bedroom so they can catch the news before getting up. It's the way we start our day. It's a ritual.

The ritual has changed. It's changed from a simple way to feed your curiosity to a ceremony of fear. Some have stopped the morning TV fix altogether, and many avoid the radio as well. Fear has become part of our national consciousness, a shared dread for what's coming next.

Anchoring a news program is considered one of the best jobs in journalism. You prepare the broadcast, work with your producers, keep yourself in mental shape, and you're watched by people across the country. It's a glamorous job and it pays well. So why are anchor people resigning? According to one famous veteran of network news, "I feel like a cop whose job is to tell people they just lost a loved one in a car accident. I feel like a daily harbinger of death."

⟞⟝

I wish I could be more philosophical, but that's not my job. Terror is my job. My name is Rick Bellamy, and I'm a 42-year-old FBI agent assigned to the Joint Terrorism Task Force in New York City. I love my work and I'm good at it. But I can't ignore the morning news. I can't ignore the radio. I can't look the other way and hope that somebody else will take care of the shit. I take a lot of Maalox.

What I do is connect dots. Dots are clues. String enough of them together and you begin to see a pattern.

I spend every waking hour looking for things that shouldn't be there and asking why things that should be there, aren't. Some people look at a bunch of scribbled lines and shrug their shoulders. I look at the same scribbles and see patterns. The first board game I ever played as a kid was *Clue,* and I always beat my parents. It stuck. I live my life looking for clues.

Recently I've seen more dots, more clues than I can ever remember, and I'm having a hard time connecting them. Maybe they're not related, maybe they're not clues, maybe there is no pattern.

Impossible – there's always a pattern, always. Just this morning I read about a suicide bombing of yet another bus in Israel. In Yemen, a bomb went off at a wedding. An elementary school in Chechnya blew up, sending 25 children to early graves. This is all familiar stuff, sickening but familiar. The only pattern I see is that none of these events involved the United States.

That was about to change.

My boss, Special FBI Agent Barbara Auletta, is a good agent. Barbara is the director of the FBI New York field office for counterterrorism. She spent her early career as a NYPD homicide detective and then joined the FBI twenty years ago. She's 55, about six feet, slim, and always well dressed. Yes, she can be tough as leather sometimes, but she's a serious professional, and treats her colleagues with respect. I've always liked her, and for some reason she likes me. Maybe it's because I pay attention when she talks, something I often forget to do with my wife Ellen.

"Rick, we're getting a fire storm of messages from headquarters."

"I've heard. Is something up?"

"That's a good question, but I don't know. It's not one thing in particular. At this point, I can't even call it a case. It's a lot of little things that we don't like. It's a lot of little dots out there that nobody can connect. That's where you come in, Sherlock. I need somebody to pick the fly shit out of the pepper."

"Can you point me in a direction, Barb?"

"A train bombing here, a gas attack there, yet another bus bombing combined with the usual reports of suicide bombings in crowds. These things are happening all over the world. The only difference is the frequency. The events are happening faster and closer together than we've ever seen. The big concern in Washington is the target of targets, Manhattan. We need to find a common element to these events."

"You mean besides jihadi scumbags?"

"Rick, that's inappropriate."

"Yes, mother, it's inappropriate. What do *you* call them?"

"Well, okay. I guess jihadi scumbags provides a starting hypothesis, but Washington is concerned that something big may be on the way. Something really big."

"Two questions, Barb. Does this investigation have a name? And will I be alone?"

"Yes and no. Its name is *Powerball* and your partner will be Agent Ezekiel Martin."

I prefer to work alone unless gunplay is involved, which it seldom is. But Zeke, as we all know him, is the perfect partner. Some agents are more concerned with their own careers and how they look in front of other agents and staff. But Zeke is a mission-driven pro. He respects my detective work and thinks of himself as a student, not just an agent. He's a 6'4" black guy with the physical skills of an athlete, having played wide receiver at the University of Michigan. Zeke is also the best marksman I've ever seen – a good guy to have your back.

"You and Zeke will meet me in my office tomorrow at 9 a.m. And Rick, this operation may be dangerous, extremely dangerous."

The events of 9/11 had become known as a Terror Spectacular, and no one old enough to remember can forget that morning. Just as people recall what they were doing when John F. Kennedy was assassinated, everyone remembers what they did when the first plane hit the World Trade Center. From the Twin Towers to the Pentagon to Shanksville, Pennsylvania, the images of destruction linger in our minds, as they were intended to.

Terrorists want to inflict fear, and 9/11 did just that. With 3,000 killed on American soil during one bright September morning at the dawn of the new century, 9/11 was *the* Terror Spectacular.

At the time the first plane hit, I was at a seminar in Quantico, Virginia, at the FBI training facility. Funny (funny?) how a traumatic event can focus your memory. Our instructor had just uttered the words 'terrorist attack' when we heard the announcement over the PA system. If I wasn't in Quantico, I would have been at my desk on the 105th floor of the North Tower. I would have been dead.

Terror has taken on a new face, a barbaric face that has every commentator searching for words.

We've started to hear a new word on the political scene, an acronym – ISIS, the Islamic State in Iraq and Syria. Even though it was founded in 1999, the term has recently become as familiar as al-Qaeda. It's also known as ISIL, for the Islamic State in the Levant, the Levant being a region including Iraq, Syria, Eastern Libya, and the Sinai Peninsula of Egypt. The most important thing about ISIS, or ISIL, are the words, *Islamic State,* an attempt by terrorist creeps to gain a political identity, not just a bunch of disaffected killers. The goal is a caliphate, a state entity run according to the Sharia Laws of Islam, a state that has no pretense toward any democratic institutions. With the constant beheadings and burning people to death, ISIS has given a new meaning to the word depravity. The subjects of an Islamic State are just that, subjects, not individuals, but human beings whose lives are controlled by a religious/political philosophy that got its start over 700 years ago.

⇒ ⇐

My job is to fight these people. It's not an easy task, or even one that's possible to define. Over my career, I've grown accustomed to dealing with all sorts of bad guys, good old-fashioned criminals who made profits selling drugs or other illegal contraband. The Mafia, for example, was easy to fight. They were driven by greed and a weird code of *omertà* , a blood oath of fealty to a strong man. Whether prostitution, drugs, or labor manipulation, the Mafia was obvious in its goals.

The world of radical Islam, on the other hand, isn't easy to figure out. Mafia types and Mexican drug lords are guided by a simple goal – to amass lots of money. Greed is an easy vice to deal with because it's easy to understand, even if you hate their goals and methods.

You can negotiate with those people, even when that negotiation might be as simple as a pre-trial plea deal. They're opportunistic and driven by material objectives – money or power or both. And you can expect them to act in predictable ways because they're self-serving.

How do you negotiate with a terrorist? How do you negotiate with someone who has nothing to negotiate? I remember the scary/funny scene in the movie *Independence Day* where the President of the United States, played by Bill Pullman, asked one of the alien invaders what they wanted us to do. "Die," was the alien's simple response. That scene keeps coming back to me. I think anyone in the military or law enforcement has the same pessimistic outlook as I have. How do you talk to somebody who wants you either dead or subjugated?

And it's getting worse, a lot worse. My chosen career is to investigate things, to look for dots and connect them to see if there's a pattern. I'm beginning to see patterns, and they're scaring the shit out of me.

CHAPTER TWO

Barbara Auletta walked into the room and poured coffee. Barbara's a good leader, and she decided to address the troops, Zeke and me.

"Al-Qaeda and ISIS," she said, "are beginning to look like predictable organizations. Before 9/11, their goals were incompatible with civilized societies, but there was at least an undercurrent of rationality that guided them. Terror works. People will eventually either bend to the demands or be killed. 9/11 changed the world. Remember how travel once had a few inconveniences, but the hassles were usually caused by bad weather or occasional bureaucratic screw-ups? Now you have to show up two hours early to catch a flight. Before 9/11, the only time you removed your shoes was if you felt a pebble."

"I hear you, Barb," I said. "It used to be a lot of basic police work, and we at least felt like we knew something was up. Then, all of a sudden, things started to change. People we call lone wolves, sole proprietors of their own terror organizations, started to show up."

"You mean like the Boston Marathon bombing?" asked Zeke.

"Yes, a perfect example," Barbara said. "a conspiracy of two people, two brothers. They simply planted bombs in satchels among the crowds of spectators. The result? Three killed, two hundred and eighty wounded. There was no organizational infrastructure, no cell phone "chatter" to alert us that something was up. Just plant a bomb and count the bodies. And what about that incident in London in 2013? A man just walked up to a British soldier and knifed him to death. The aftermath was on video for the world to see. The killer, covered in blood, calmly explained to the camera why he murdered in the name of Islam. He was just one man. There was no evidence of activities that could have alerted law enforcement. One knife, one corpse. And last October a man walked up to two cops right here in New York City. He took an ax from under his coat and started swinging, hitting one cop in the back of the head, almost killing the guy."

"Barb," I said, "how do you connect dots when there are no dots? How do you know when a lone actor bursts forth with his own little jihad? How do you stop a guy who wants to die, even if you know what he's up to? How do you get between a lone wolf and his prey?"

Barbara put her face in her hands and shook her head.

That's where I come in. One of the reasons I'm a good investigator is that I obsess over solving a case. But lately I've felt like a blind man asked to look at nothing and describe what he saw.

"And how the hell is a lone wolf even a dot?" asked Zeke. "An investigative dot, by definition, is something you know about. So a guy attacks a cop with a hatchet. Fine, a dot, a hatchet-wielding nut. So now what? Every time we see one of these incidents, we try to find out as much as possible about the assailant. That's obvious. And the one thing we find all the time is evidence of Islamic radicalism in the guy's background."

"And the guy with the ax even had a Facebook page with radical rants all over it," I said. "That man was actually on our watch list. So what? Do we round up everybody who has radical postings on social media? Of course we don't. Even if the Constitution allowed us to do such a thing, which it doesn't, would we really want to live in a country where people could be locked up for their beliefs? So we have a radical who posted his ideas on Facebook for the world to see. It doesn't take too long for one nut to pick up one ax and start swinging."

"Guys," said Barbara, "Washington thinks that something big is coming. I can't say why, but I think they're right."

CHAPTER THREE

Ellen and I were having breakfast at our kitchen table as usual at 6 a.m. We used to go out for breakfast all the time, but we realized we usually weren't that hungry in the morning and would only wind up eating a lot of fatty foods. I love starting my day talking to Ellen because that's the time of day I'm able to follow what she's saying – a time before my brain fills up with a case I'm working on. Our conversation turned to a new big assignment Ellen had just landed. For some crazy reason, Ellen gets horny as hell when she lands a big architectural commission, and she just had. Maybe I should help her do some marketing to land more big jobs.

"So tell me more about this big assignment, honey. I can tell you're all excited."

Ellen smiled, winked, and squeezed my knee.

"It's a super job, probably the biggest I've ever handled. The client, Angus MacPherson, is filthy rich. He owns shopping malls across the country and is gobbling up land to build more. He's an interesting guy. He's over six feet tall, around seventy years old, and has an explosion of white hair. He's an American citizen, but he speaks with a Scottish brogue so thick you could cut it with a plastic knife. I've never met a client who has more input into a project. He's leaving the design details to me, but he has some specific requirements that I find strange."

"Strange?" I asked. That word always gets my attention. Something that's strange means that it's something that shouldn't be there. And something that shouldn't be there often turns out to be a dot.

"Yeah, strange," said Ellen. "Instead of a second or third floor, he wants each shopping center to have only one floor, with huge stainless steel ceiling panels tilted inward. The entire ceiling will actually be stainless steel. I've done preliminary sketches, and the design looks beautiful, but it doesn't make sense. What do you think, Rick?"

"I think you're right. Strange is the word. How much rentable floor space is this man giving up just for a pretty design? Is he a businessman or an art lover?"

"I'll give you a specific number, Rick. For the first five shopping centers he's planning, he'll give up over 90,000 square feet of retail space. At the average rental prices in the five different markets, he'll lose a potential $3.6 million a year, just on the first five projects."

"This is wrong," I said. "This is just plain fucked up. Sorry for my language, hon, but nobody who calls himself a businessman would sacrifice that kind of money just for an aesthetically pleasing design. Ellen, I want you to keep me up to date on these projects. Something is out of place."

"Are you talking as my husband or an FBI agent? I wouldn't be happy if you found something wrong and locked up my favorite client. This project is so exciting."

"Does that mean you're going to feel frisky for the life of the job?"

"Yes, it probably does." She leaned over and kissed me.

"In that case, if I find he's in violation of the law, I won't bust him until the last possible moment."

Finally, we found something about Ellen's job that I could focus on, something that would make me pay more attention to what she was saying, something new for me to obsess about.

Could Angus MacPherson be a new dot? I had no idea, but Ellen's numbers told me this project didn't make sense. And things that don't make sense often show up as a case file.

What was about to happen didn't make sense either.

After breakfast with Ellen I walked to my office at 26 Federal Plaza in lower Manhattan, about 10 minutes from our apartment in Greenwich Village. It was a brisk October 15, perfect for a walk. My office was quiet in the early morning, and I sat with a cup of decaf – I limit myself to decaf after having no more than full-strength cups of coffee. My nervous system was already on full alert as a matter of course, so why make it any more jittery. I opened a file and started to go into my zone, the zone of suspicion and dot connecting. I'd gotten into the habit over the years of disbelieving everything, a useful mindset for a detective. That makes Ellen nervous, although I keep assuring her that my suspicious nature doesn't include people I love, especially her.

My case involved the recent ax attack on a New York City cop. As usual, the dots were all there, except nobody saw them until the event happened. The guy was a denizen of various nasty forums and chat rooms on the Internet, all specializing in a rabid form of Islamic radicalism. What drives me crazy is that I can't understand the hatred. I've studied everything I could get my hands on about the growth of a radical personality, the religious views, the politics, the desire for the "end of days," a final cataclysm that will bring the forces of extreme Islam into direct clash with the West, a Hollywood-style explosion where all the bad guys (us) are defeated. Fine, I got it. But I really don't. I understand it intellectually, but I don't get it in my gut. Until I do, I'll be just a researcher, not an investigator.

My thoughts were suddenly broken when Barbara Auletta charged into my office, slamming the door against the wall.

"Good morning, Barbara, nice to see you too."

"Don't be a wise ass," she said – a pretty tall order – as she grabbed the remote and clicked it at the TV in the corner of my office.

Wolf Blitzer, the CNN anchor, appeared on the screen, wearing his trademarked "look of concern." The camera panned to what looked like the scene of a bombing. Bodies littered the ground in front of a typical mid-Manhattan office building. The camera quickly panned away from the bodies, a blessed bow to viewer sensitivity by the CNN execs. You can tell the public about gore and mayhem, but you don't have to show it.

Matthew Jenkins, the reporter on the scene, looked like he was in shock. So did Barbara. I guess I did too.

"For our viewers who have just tuned in, behind me you can see the devastation that occurred less than 20 minutes ago. From what we have learned, a lone suicide bomber detonated a heavy explosive device at the entrance lobby to 666 Fifth Avenue, one of Manhattan's most prominent office buildings. Of course, at this early stage in the story, I have no idea of the identity of the bomber or his motive. I don't believe I'm going out on a limb to say that we suspect terrorism. Suicide bombers and terror go together. But of course we can't say it was definitely a terrorist act until we know more. Back to you, Wolf."

I checked my jacket pocket to make sure I had a couple of extra clips for my Glock, then stood and walked toward the door.

"Stay put for a few minutes, Rick," said Barbara. "It's chaos out there now, and the NYPD is on the scene. Let's learn as much as we can from CNN. As of right now, the news people know more than we do. Sometimes these guys make our jobs easier."

Blitzer reappeared on the TV and he began to speak, but before he could get two words out, he grabbed his ear and said, "Oh, my God."

Blitzer's a pro, and he seldom shows emotion on screen, but it was obvious that a producer had just filled his ear with some more news, some bad news.

"I've just received word that there has been another bombing, this time on Wall Street, apparently in front of the New York Stock Exchange. We go now to Pam Rickman, our CNN reporter on the scene."

A shot of the front the New York Stock Exchange appeared on the screen.

"Wolf," said Rickman, "the scene here is horrific. It's 8:45 a.m. and Wall Street is its normal mass of humanity. Whoever pulled this off was obviously looking for the maximum number of casualties. Right now, we think it was a lone suicide bomber. Three deaths have been confirmed, but, and I hate to say it, that toll is probably going to rise throughout the day. We don't want to show the direct shots of the scene because, frankly, it's too horrible. I can tell you that I see about 20 people lying on the pavement. How many are dead or severely wounded is something we don't know at this point."

Blitzer peppered her with questions, most of which she had no answers for yet.

As Barbara and I stared at the TV, we suddenly rose two inches off the floor. The windows of my office shattered, following the loudest explosion I'd heard since my tour with the Marines in Iraq. When we landed we both fell sideways, and Barbara slammed her head against the corner of my desk. I didn't think, I just let my Marine and FBI training take over. My office was a danger zone, and we had to get us out of there. Barbara was conscious but bleeding heavily from the left side of her scalp. I asked if she could walk on her own. She stared at me, not hearing a word I said. I picked her up and carried her into the hallway.

"We need medical help here," I yelled. Within minutes a couple of EMTs from our medical department ran down the hall. One of them kneeled next to the director to assess her injuries. Barbara, one tough lady, actually smiled and made a thumbs up sign.

Zeke Martin came running down the hall. My ears were still ringing, but I slowly regained my hearing.

"The bomb went off in the lobby," said Zeke. "I think we lost a lot of people. The building is on lockdown and security wants us to stay on this floor. Let's go into the conference room so we can leave the hallway open."

The EMTs put Barbara into a wheelchair and moved her into the room with Zeke and me. She apparently did not have a concussion, just a nasty superficial gash on her head.

"Here's what we know and it's not a lot," said Zeke. "The first bomb was at 666 Fifth Avenue, followed by the New York Stock Exchange five minutes later, and our building five minutes after that."

Zeke clicked on the TV in the conference room as he looked at his watch. Fortunately the TV still worked after the explosion on the first floor.

"By my count we have one minute until the next five-minute mark. Let's see what Blitzer has to say."

Exactly at the five-minute mark, Blitzer held his hand to his ear and looked at the TV camera.

"Our nation is under attack," said Blitzer. "I've just received word from our affiliate in Boston that a bomb has exploded at the entrance to Faneuil Hall, the crowded marketplace. That's the fourth bombing in 20 minutes."

NYC Mayor de Blasio appeared on the TV. He said he was in contact with the Transit Authority and all commuter railroads. He had ordered outbound trains to return to the city to bring commuters home.

Until further notification, New York City was closed for business. What we all feared would happen was happening.

⇥⇤

Six more senior agents filed into the conference room across the hall from my wrecked office. Director Auletta, whack on the head or not, knew she had to address her people.

"We've thought about this," said Barbara. "We studied it, we war-gamed it, and we obsessed over it. Well, it's happening. Lone wolves are attacking our country. It seemed too easy. Each suicide bomber had a simple job. All he needed was a suicide vest, a location, and a time. Nothing high-tech, nothing that required a lot of planning, nothing that required a lot of chatter. Just a bomb vest, a location, and a time. And a person willing to give up his life."

Zeke looked at his watch and raised his hand.

"We're almost at the next five-minute-mark, director."

Auletta pointed the remote at the TV and increased the volume. She had switched stations to get another point of view.

"This is Shepard Smith of Fox News, ladies and gentlemen. It sickens me to tell you that we've just received word that a bomb detonated in front of the FBI building in Washington. We've been told that a man in an overcoat approached the building, and when he refused orders to stop, the police opened fire, but not before he detonated the bomb. Three officers are down and we don't have details on their condition at this time. We go now to the White House, where President Reynolds is about to address the nation."

William Reynolds, the President of the United States, appeared on the screen.

"This is the worst morning our nation has faced since the attacks of 9/11," said Reynolds. "But we have contingency plans which we've shared with military and law enforcement agencies across the country. Until further notice, no one shall enter any building carrying a briefcase or package at any time until that person has submitted to a search. If you wear an overcoat, you must remove it for inspection. After a conference call with the governors of all states, I inform you that the National Guard has been mobilized in every state to assist with law enforcement. These measures will be a burden, but I call on the American people to recognize that we are faced with a national emergency, one that requires extreme vigilance and some hard decisions. That is all for now. Together we will get through this trying time. God bless you and God bless America."

In times of danger and chaos, the job of the Commander in Chief is to sooth nerves and calm fears. He had a tough job that morning because he didn't know what the hell was happening any more than the rest of us. It wasn't a Winston Churchill speech, but what more could the guy say? We were under attack and we didn't know how bad it was going to be.

"Okay folks, we get paid to think and act, not to panic," said Director Auletta, holding a cold compress to the cut on her head. "I need your thoughts."

I raised my hand but put it down quickly because I noticed it was shaking. I like to think of myself as a tough guy, a Marine combat veteran and a pistol-packing FBI agent. But I didn't feel tough. I felt like a scared kid.

"I don't think we've seen the end of this," I said. "I think they're working the clock, picking the timing to ensure the maximum number of casualties – rush hour, as people are pouring into buildings on their way to work. What really scares me is that this is worse than 9/11. Remember Mayor Giuliani cheering everybody to go out to a show, to go shopping, to get on with their lives? But this is different. How do people get on with their lives when they expect another bomb to go off – anywhere?"

"Do you think the worst of it is over, Rick?" said Auletta.

"I do, but five minutes haven't passed yet."

Zeke looked at his watch.

"Everybody, look at the TV," yelled Zeke.

"This is Shepard Smith reporting for Fox News."

He held his ear, wearing a face that looked like fear itself, not the calm demeanor of a seasoned anchorman.

"I'm getting a carload of reports, ladies and gentlemen. I've just been told that there has been a train derailment on the New York Metro North line at the Spuyten Duyvil station in Riverdale. We have an unconfirmed report that an explosion ripped through the first car as it pulled out of the station. A few cars derailed and fell into Spuyten Duyvil Creek, a part of the Hudson River. I also have information that a Long Island Railroad train has been derailed near Garden City as it approached the station. There was also an explosion before the derailment. Oh, Dear Lord, folks. I'm now hearing that an Acela commuter train has exploded and derailed as it traveled through New London, Connecticut."

The network graphic people worked furiously to make sense of the overload of data that was spewing into Smith's ear. He walked over to a video monitor, which showed the train wrecks as soon as they were reported.

"Folks, I was on the air when the 9/11 attacks occurred. I have to tell you that this morning's news makes 9/11 look like just another story. The Fox producers are giving my ear a break, and our graphics people are listing the train derailments as they receive the reports."

Smith walked over to the huge monitor, shaking his head as one report after another flashed on the screen.

"You're seeing the events as they happen, folks.

- Washington, D.C. Metro near Arlington, Virginia. Seven cars derailed.
- Chicago Transit Authority train was thrown off the tracks in the Loop with five cars plummeting to East Wacker Drive.
- A Bay Area Rapid Transit train was derailed near Mission Street in San Francisco with eight cars involved.
- A New York subway train exploded and derailed underground at the 42nd Street station, one of the busiest in New York, as it was packed with morning commuters.
- These are in addition to the explosions at Spuyten Duyvil, the Long Island Railroad in Garden City, and the Acela in New London, Connecticut.

"Unlike the building attacks that I reported just a short while ago, these train derailments appear to have been simultaneous," said Smith, "As best as we can make out from the reports, all of the train explosions occurred at 9:37 a.m. Eastern Time. It's now 10 a.m. and we haven't received any further reports. Needless to say, we will be reporting the aftermath of these disasters throughout the day with no commercial interruptions."

⇥ ⇤

"Rick," said Barbara, still holding a cold compress against the cut on her scalp, "assemble your team in the Communications Room. I'll be there with you. We have more dots to connect than we ever imagined. Okay, everybody, I know you'd like to try to contact your families. We have our secure cell phone network, so chances are you may be able to get through. But I have no idea how our loved ones' phones will work. Let's take a half-hour break. I just pray to God that we've heard the end of this."

I called Ellen's cell number, and I couldn't believe she picked up after only two rings.

"Where are you, hon?" I said.

"I'm still in our apartment. Remember, I had to wait for the plumber for that clogged sink?"

"Stay put, Ellen. Nobody knows what the hell is going on, and I don't want you going into any buildings."

"I need to see you, Rick."

"I understand, honey. I wish you were with me right now."

"No. I mean, yeah, being with you sounds great, but I need to talk to you about my new client."

"Now? I can't possibly focus on anything but the attacks of this morning."

"Rick, I've been researching this guy. You told me to keep you up to date. There's some stuff you absolutely need to know – *now*. If I walk I can be at your office in 10 minutes. The subways are shut down and forget trying to catch a cab."

"Can you give me a hint about what you've found out?"

"No, I don't think we should talk about it on the phone. I'll see you in 10 minutes."

Ellen was about to drop another bomb in my lap.

Zeke, three others from my team, and I met with Barbara Auletta in what we called the Communications Room, a place designed for quick response to unfolding situations. The other members of the team included agents Michele Hannon, Phil Lopez, and Mike Turner. Information about the suspects came in. Unless there was a surveillance photo or an eyewitness, we wouldn't know anything about the bombers' identities. We were plugged into the FBI's gigantic databank of suspected terrorists with background information and photographs.

Fortunately, most office buildings have surveillance cameras facing the entrances. The trains, on the other hand, were more difficult. Almost all train platforms have cameras but there are none inside most of the trains. So we were looking for people carrying a bag or briefcase or who wore bulky clothing.

Zeke has a mind like an Oracle database, so his job was to sort the possible identities as they came in.

We had five building bombers and seven train bombers to identify.

Zeke stood at the flipchart and wrote the names of the suspects, one by one. Nobody said it, but we all expected to see men in their 20s or 30s with swarthy complexions and Arabic names. Political correctness and good investigative work don't go together. We were all mentally profiling.

"Dolores Abernathy," said Zeke, "suspected bomber of the New York Stock Exchange. In this video, you can see her looking around and then pulling a cord on her coat. When we slow down the video, we can see that the blast came from her body. Here's what we know. She was 25 years old, of Irish and German heritage, went to Catholic schools right through college. When she was 21 years old, she was arrested and convicted on an aggravated assault charge for swinging a bat at a cop during a peace rally. She converted to Islam during her 30 days in jail, and her Islamic name is Fatima Chatwa. She's been on our watch list since then.

"Timothy Lavaro is suspected of bombing the building we're sitting in, based on the video. He was 23 years old. Both parents are Italian. He was convicted of drug dealing three times and was on parole. We have no documentary evidence about his religion, but his Facebook page shows an Arabic message, translated as, 'All Infidels must die.' In 2008 he travelled to Syria.

"I'm going to step back for a moment," said Zeke, "and give you a rundown on the 12 suspects we think we have a handle on. You may want to take a sip of water before I go any further.

"Of the 12," Zeke said, "not one is of Middle Eastern descent. All are between the ages of 21 and 29. Five, count 'em *five*, are women. And this is interesting. Every one of them is Caucasian. I keep telling you folks that white people can't be trusted."

"Very funny, wise guy, said Director Auletta. "Great work as usual, Zeke. Let me interject a couple of observations. Ever since ISIS split off from al-Qaeda, we've watched this phenomenon known as 'homegrown terrorists.' Since last year Western authorities have identified dozens of

Muslim converts who travelled to Syria or Iraq to learn how to wage jihad. A lot of Americans fit the description of a homegrown jihadi. What Zeke just showed us is the new face of terror, the new face of radicalism, the new war. This morning's events tell us one thing – it's no longer business as usual in this fight. Gone are the days of profiling, the days when we searched for guys who look like Mohammed Atta. The new enemy could be sitting next to us on a bus or a plane. I'm not sure what this means, at least not yet anyway. Does it mean that cops will stop and frisk people at random? Does it mean people can't wear bulky coats or carry packages? I hope you all saw something that I noticed looking at the videos. The suicide bomb vests are a lot slimmer than they used to be. So far, I didn't see a person wearing a coat or jacket that I could describe as bulky."

"Director, if I may interject," I said. (I never call her Barbara in public.) "As Zeke pointed out, 11 of the 12 people we've ID'd so far are on our watch list. We may have to tighten up on our surveillance."

"Rick," said Auletta, "after what I've seen this morning, my inclination is to shove a tracking device up the ass of anyone we have suspicions about. But, of course, we live in the land of the

United States Constitution. So we see this guy, Timothy Lavaro, with his radical Facebook postings. Maybe it should raise some eyebrows, but what he did was perfectly legal. Do we assign an agent to physically track anybody we suspect as a radical? Sorry, guys, but as FBI agents we know it's our job to think out of the box, as difficult as that may be. And now, we have a new friggin box."

We heard a knock on the door. I opened it and an assistant said, "Mrs. Bellamy is here to see you, sir."

I had alerted everybody that Ellen would be meeting with us. What Ellen had to tell us would blow our minds as much as Zeke's presentation.

Meeting be damned, I walked up to Ellen and wrapped my arms around her. We kissed, probably far too long for the circumstances, but I was consumed by the fact that she was okay.

Everybody in the room knew Ellen from our many social outings. Ellen and Barbara Auletta are good friends.

"You guys look like hammered dog poop, if you don't mind an independent critique," said Ellen.

We all laughed. Ellen has a way with people.

"Rick tells us you may have some useful information, Ellen," said Auletta.

"Yes, but I'm feeling a little uncomfortable. This is an official meeting, and I'm just an everyday civilian without a security clearance."

"Hon," I said, "remember, for better or worse, that you married an FBI agent. The FBI knows more about you than you know about yourself. Standard practice when an agent gets married."

"Well that makes me feel comfortable," Ellen said, "sort of like a microbe on a Petri dish."

"Don't sweat it Ellen," said Barbara. "Every one of our spouses went through the same wringer. And if it makes you feel better, because the FBI knows so much about you, I'm hereby appointing you as Special Deputy Ellen Bellamy, FBI. You'll get a stipend, but just don't expect health benefits or a pension."

"In that case, I think I'll take some advance pay with one of those sandwiches over there. I haven't had lunch yet."

Auletta apologized for our lack of hospitality. She asked Zeke to summarize his report to bring Ellen up to speed.

⊫ ⊨

When Ellen finished her sandwich, she opened a large file and took out its contents.

"Rick and I were talking about the newest architectural assignment that I recently landed. I was all excited. Whenever I get a large project I..."

I coughed loudly and stared at Ellen. I hoped she wasn't going to tell them how horny she gets when she lands a big project.

Ellen looked at me, winked, and continued.

"My passion is large projects. I get, well, fulfilled." She winked at me again. "Rick was a little shaken by some things I told him about a Mr. Angus MacPherson, the head of MacPherson International. I'll go into detail about the strange shopping center designs he wants me to work on, but first I want you to know about some other interesting things I've learned recently. The past few hours of hell made me think."

Ellen was about to deliver an electric shock to our meeting.

"How did you come to meet this Mr. MacPherson, Ellen?" asked Auletta.

"He called me out of the blue. I had just won an award from *Architectural Digest* for a shopping center I worked on in Minneapolis. I guess he was impressed with the design. He asked me to meet him at his office on Park Avenue. That was eight months ago. Since then I've come up with the preliminary design and drawings for all of the shopping centers. Rick agrees with me that the designs make no sense from a business point of view. MacPherson seems to want to sacrifice a ton of retail space and rental income for aesthetic reasons."

Ellen walked over to a cork board on the wall and tacked up one of the drawings.

"Notice how the ceiling panels are all sloped inward. I recommended standard sheetrock for the construction, but MacPherson insists that they be made of stainless steel. Although it will be beautiful, it will cost a fortune."

"But what's wrong with a wealthy guy blowing his money?" asked Agent Michele Hannon. "Fat cats spend fortunes all the time to create a legacy for themselves."

"That's a possibility, Michele," I said, "but this guy is well known as a smart investor. Hey, it's possible that he's suddenly become an artiste, but I look at it as a possible red light – a possible dot. I have no idea why at this point, but it's something we should be aware of. Ellen, you said that you found some other interesting stuff."

"Yes, and I'm not sure what it means. MacPherson, you may be surprised to know, is the nation's biggest investor in security firms. Either through his own company, MacPherson International, or through holding companies, he controls the majority of private security companies in the nation. That includes any airports that aren't manned by TSA agents. If it's private, chances are 90 percent that it's controlled by MacPherson."

"What are your thoughts on this Ellen?" asked Auletta. "You have my full attention when I hear that something as critical as security is controlled by one man, but why do you find this strange?"

"Vertical integration is the answer, Madam Director. He also owns or controls most of the suppliers for the projects. Before I turned to architecture, I was trained in business. I have an MBA from Wharton, not to brag, but to show you that I know what I'm talking about. Just as the sloping ceiling panels in the shopping centers make no sense, neither does his control of the vast majority of subcontractors. You'd expect him to farm out the work. It may seem like a good idea, but when you drill down, it doesn't stack up economically. A developer like this would normally let out projects for bids, opting to pay fees as needed rather than keep a huge payroll with health insurance and pension costs. But he controls everything, including hiring and firing."

"Does any of this connect with the bombings this morning?" asked Zeke.

"All I know are the facts, Zeke," said Ellen. "MacPherson owned the security firms that worked all the railroad and transit lines that were hit this morning."

"Holy shit," Zeke said.

"How could that be?" asked Auletta. "The Metropolitan Transit Authority provides security here in New York."

"You would think so. But in the past four years, because of municipal budget cuts, transportation agencies across the country have farmed out part of their security to private bidders. I haven't researched it yet, but I wouldn't be surprised if the private buildings that were bombed this morning all had MacPherson-supplied security."

Ellen was freaking me out. How did she know this stuff, and why didn't she ever mention it to me? She seemed to know what I was thinking. Come to think of it, maybe she did tell me but, as usual, I wasn't listening to her.

"I became fascinated with the workings of MacPherson International," Ellen said. "I never even mentioned it to Rick because I couldn't see anything suspicious, just strange business decisions. As I watched the horrible news this morning, it suddenly dawned on me. I don't know if this means anything, but Rick always says that when things aren't the way they're supposed to be, they could be clues to something bigger. I guess my detective husband is rubbing off on me."

"Big question, Ellen," said Agent Lopez, "how did you find out about all this?"

"It's all hidden in plain sight on the Internet."

"Rick," said Auletta, "I'm assigning you to investigate MacPherson International. Ellen and Zeke will be on your team. Find out whatever you can about the mysterious Mr. MacPherson and his companies. Ellen, do you have a problem investigating a client?"

"No, I don't. This could all amount to nothing, but if there's any connection between MacPherson and terror, I'm all aboard to do whatever I can."

Ellen's on to something, I thought, something interesting.

CHAPTER FOUR

It was November 5 – three weeks since the bombings of October 15. Already "10/15" had become a sad part of the American lexicon, right up there with 9/11.

Ellen, Zeke, and I scoured every bit of information about MacPherson International. We looked at reports from securities analysts, magazines articles, and even a book entitled, *Angus MacPherson, The Scottish Bill Gates*. Zeke and I interviewed a dozen security heads from the various MacPherson firms. We told them it was a routine check. Not one of the people we interviewed gave any hint that something was amiss. We then investigated each of the people we interviewed. Nothing out of the ordinary.

After three weeks of intense investigation, we had nothing on MacPherson that even hinted at wrongdoing. It seemed that MacPherson is an incredibly talented businessman, but the only pieces that still didn't fit were the strange designs for the shopping centers. Ellen told us that MacPherson wants to open the five malls on the day after Thanksgiving, next year, Black Friday. That makes perfect sense. If you're going to launch a retail project, doing so on the busiest shopping day of the year is simply good business.

I interviewed a stock analyst who convinced me that owning the security companies that guard your businesses could be a sound move, although he agreed with Ellen that it was out of the ordinary.

MacPherson was clean. But something in my gut told me not to close the file.

The MacPherson shopping mall plans still didn't make any sense. We'd soon find out why.

CHAPTER FIVE

After three weeks, Ellen and I took what seemed like our only break since the attacks. We sat on the sofa sipping wine after a light dinner.

If there's any such thing as objective beauty, Ellen is it. She's 38 years old, 5'9," blonde, with an amazing body that she keeps in shape with her daily workout. And she isn't just physically beautiful. She has a kindness about her for everybody she comes into contact with. She isn't just kind, she's patient – a handy trait if you live with me. She's an award-winning architect and smart as hell. Sounds corny perhaps, but Ellen is also my best friend. I think she feels that way about me too.

"Just hold me, Rick. We haven't talked about it much, but when I heard the FBI building was bombed, I thought I'd die. When you finally reached me on my cell phone, I felt like I got a new life. Also, I notice that you're listening more to what I have to say. Have I mentioned how much I love you?"

"It's been a few minutes, hon, but I never tire of hearing it."

"So where the hell are we now, Rick? It looks like my MacPherson suspicions were just that, suspicions with nothing to go on."

"As I said, babe, I'm not closing the MacPherson file. Here's where we are, in answer to your question. In less than an hour on 10/15, a bunch of suicidal creeps have changed American life. That's the simple answer."

"Rick, do you really think our lives have changed?"

"Hey, look around. Ridership on public transportation has shrunk to a trickle. The mayor has banned private cars in the city unless they're occupied by at least four people. I spoke to my cousin yesterday, the guy who's in the telecommunications business. He says that his business is booming so much he can't hire people fast enough to keep up with the demand. It seems that American companies are finally looking at telecommuting as the normal way of doing business, not just an alternative for blizzards and hurricanes. Before anybody enters a building, they have to submit to a search. After 9/11 it was just airplanes. Now it's a nightmare just trying to get to work."

"I've noticed. I wish I had an FBI badge like you."

"Forget the badge. I wish you had a gun. As a matter of fact, I want you to get a concealed carry permit. You're my wife and you're also a prominent architect. I hate to think of you as a target, but I don't want to take any chances. I also want you to get checked out on an assault rifle. I know a guy in the NYPD who can move the paperwork fast."

"I can't believe that less than a month ago I would never have thought to carry a gun, but I think you have a point, Rick. I still hate the idea."

"I have to go to a meeting at FBI headquarters in D.C. on Tuesday. I'll feel a lot better when you're armed. I can train you on how to use the guns."

"How romantic. 'So what did you and Rick do for the weekend? Oh, the usual. We went to the shooting range.' "

"To change the subject," I said, "I can use a shower. It's been a stressful day."

"I have a couple of new yoga positions to show you," she said.

"In the shower?"

"Why not?"

"Can I have a clue?"

"I'd rather let you connect the dots."

CHAPTER SIX

Sarah Watson, Director of the FBI, called a meeting with Barbara Auletta, Zeke, and me at FBI headquarters in Washington. It was November 11, and we were still trying to discover anything we could about the bombings of 10/15.

When we walked into Watson's office, I was surprised to see William Carlini, Director of the CIA, along with a tall Middle Eastern-looking guy who I had never met.

"Folks," Watson said, "it's my pleasure to introduce CIA Director Bill Carlini, a man who I know you recognize. Next to Director Carlini is CIA Agent Charles Atkins, also known as Gamal Akhbar, also known as a bunch of other names. We call him Buster. I'm going to summarize what we know about the bombings of 10/15, which isn't a hell of a lot. Of the 12 terrorist bombers, we have a positive ID on 11 of them, which is pretty good. But we find ourselves in uncharted waters. After every terror investigation, we expect to find a lot of Middle Eastern names. But we've found none. They are all "homegrown" fanatics, recruited by God knows who, people who exchanged their status as American citizens for the cause of radical jihad. I'm going to ask Director Carlini to fill you in on Buster."

"Good morning," said Carlini. "You've never heard of Agent Atkins before, and that's the way we like it. Buster, in my somewhat informed opinion, is the best spy in the CIA, and one of the quickest thinkers I ever met. I've made no secret about my recommendation of Buster to replace me when I eventually retire. I'm going to turn this meeting over to Buster, who is going to share his thoughts with us."

Buster stood to address us. He was a tall, good looking guy with a swarthy complexion. He had broad shoulders and stood with the posture of a Marine.

"Hello, folks, it's my pleasure to meet you. From my physical appearance, you may think I rode in on a camel. I'm a jihad's worst nightmare. I look like I live in a tent, but I'm American. I'm a Coptic Christian, my mother having been born in Lebanon, and that's where I get my Arabian looks. I was born and raised in Brooklyn, as you may tell from my Arabic accent."

We all laughed. This guy may be tough, but he was also easy to like.

A guard escorted a short bald man wearing a gray pin striped suit into the room.

"I'm sorry I'm late, folks. There was a wicked accident on the Beltway."

"It's my pleasure to introduce Dr. Benjamin Weinberg," said Director Watson. "Ben is a psychiatrist and detective with the New York City Police Department. He's worked with the FBI on so many cases I'm trying to convince him to join us full time. Bennie, as he likes to be called, is a nationally famous expert on detecting lies from witnesses. He's a hit with prosecutors, both state and federal. Bennie carries a card that reads, 'Bennie the Bullshit Detector.' He's also an uncanny observer of human behavior. Buster, please continue."

Buster walked over to Bennie and they smiled and shook hands. These two were obviously old friends.

"Director Watson hit the nail on the head when she said we're in uncharted waters," said Buster. "Whenever we investigate a terrorist incident, we expect to find somebody who looks like me. But 10/15 opened a new chapter in the story. Not one of the 12 people we identified was Middle Eastern. We've sifted through the available background information on each of them, and we see one thing in common. They all, at some point in their lives, became enthralled with the idea of radical Islam. We also know that 10/15 wasn't a bunch of lone wolf operations. The way the bombings were executed tells us there was command and control. But even though there was coordination, the operation was simple, and that's why there was none of the familiar 'chatter' leading up to the date. A suicide vest, a set time, a set place, and a human being willing to kill himself – or herself – in the name of a perverted ideology that traffics as religion. But there's another thing about this incident that concerns us. I'm going to use the term 'self-radicalized,' meaning that these people weren't brainwashed, but washed their own brains. I'm going to ask Dr. Bennie to weigh in."

"You're all probably thinking," said Bennie, "that no person in his right mind would do such a thing. And you'd be right. None of these people were in their right minds, but that doesn't mean they were clinically insane. The best area for us to focus on is the act of suicide itself. Studies have shown, including some of my own papers on the subject, that people who commit suicide come from all economic levels but primarily from comfortable circumstances. That pattern fits the killers of 10/15. They probably would have turned up as suicides without killing other people, but radical Islam gave them something irresistible, a chance to go out in what the killer perceives as a flash of glory, a chance to make something out of a meaningless life. Some may have turned in this direction by a spurned lover, a tyrannical boss, or an argument with a neighbor. It sounds so mundane, and that's the scary part about this. We can't go around interrogating people to find out if they're unhappy with their lives or if there is a family history of suicide. Even if we could come up with a group of suspects based on a psychological profile, then what? Imagine a world where a cop says, 'You're under arrest on suspicion of being a disaffected loner with no enjoyment of life.' I've been in law enforcement for a long time, and we know that ain't gonna happen, not that we want it to. I hate to sound negative, but getting blown up by a suicide bomber is just one of life's risks, and after 10/15, it's something we may need to learn to live with – or die with."

"Bennie," said Director Watson, "are you saying there was no way we could have stopped 10/15?"

"Well, it's conceivable that we could have stopped it, but only for one reason – this wasn't a lone wolf operation. There was command and control, somebody who called the shots, somebody who picked the targets, rounded up the jihadis, and set the times. Did we miss any clues? After 9/11 we saw all sorts of clues, all sorts of missed opportunities. But 9/11 was a different beast. It was a carefully orchestrated and complicated terror spectacular. The 10/15 incidents were part of a simple operation – a lot of parts, but simple. We've said it before – a time, a place, a bomb vest, and a detonator. If we missed any clues I have no idea, probably because I don't have a need to know. Maybe Buster or one of you FBI folks can answer that."

"I can answer that," said Watson. "For the past month we've looked at little else beyond trying to unravel this mess. I've spent countless hours on the phone with Director Carlini here, and I can say this with certainty – we didn't have a clue. Even if we missed some obvious evidence and some operative tried to cover his ass by not pointing it out after the fact, I can say there were no

clues, no hints, no dots. Both the FBI and the CIA have the same procedure when doing a post-mortem of an event. All agents are urged to submit a list of things that we missed – anonymously. The sorry state of affairs is that 10/15 came as a total surprise. A big spectacular, but a simple spectacular."

"Buster," said Carlini, "I've seen you pull a lot of rabbits out of a lot of hats over the years. In your opinion, can another attack like this be prevented?"

"The simple answer is yes, it can be prevented. Beyond that, I don't want to say anything except to you, Mr. Director. Sorry folks, but once a spook, always a spook. Until the time comes to open it, I keep my mouth shut. All I can say at this point is that my team and I are working on it."

"Rick, I'm assigning Buster to work with you and your team," said Director Carlini. "I've already discussed it with Director Watson and Barbara Auletta. The old bullshit days of the CIA and FBI not cooperating have changed since 9/11. After 10/15, I'm declaring it officially dead."

From what I learned about Buster, I was happy to have him on my team. I wondered how he got the nickname Buster.

I'd find out soon.

CHAPTER SEVEN

"Mr. MacPherson will see you now, Mrs. Bellamy," said Angus MacPherson's assistant. She had a heavy accent of some sort that I couldn't place.

This was my first meeting with MacPherson in a month. The shopping center project was well under way, and I saw no problem with his projected launch date of the day after Thanksgiving next year, Black Friday.

His office was what you'd expect for a man of such wealth. It was large, about 30 feet by 40 feet. The view of Manhattan was breathtaking from his 40th floor office on Park Avenue. In the middle of the office was a large conference table. As a real estate developer, he spent a lot of time hovering over plans and charts. The smell of the leather furniture gave off a hint of power. Photographs of his various real estate developments from all over the world covered the walls.

"Ellen, lassie, good to see ya. Please have a seat."

MacPherson's Scottish brogue was charming. He always calls me "lassie." He's a tall man, about 6'3" and heavy set. He was elegantly dressed in a Savile Row tweed suit. MacPherson is 70 years old, with a shock of white hair that set him apart from the dark surrounding walls.

"It's good to see you too, Mr. MacPherson."

"Call me Angus, lassie. Don't make me feel old. Tell me, how did you weather the recent storm of October 15?"

"No problems, Angus, except for the shock that everyone felt that day. And is everything okay with you?"

"The only impact on MacPherson International was the small army of FBI agents who wanted to know everything about my security business. Just doing their jobs, of course, but it was an annoyance."

Of course I didn't mention that my husband was in charge of the investigation.

"So tell me, lass, how are the plans coming along?"

We stood and walked over to the conference table where I spread out the latest drawings. As we went over the details Angus asked the kind of perceptive questions you'd expect from such a successful developer. Most of his questions concerned the sloping stainless steel ceilings.

"Tell me, Ellen, what is your personal opinion of the plans? I know that I may have stepped all over your architect's sensitivity with my specifications. Be honest with me, lass."

"I'll be perfectly honest with you, Angus. I've said it before and I'll repeat it now. The sloped ceilings eliminate a second, or in a couple of the buildings, a third floor retail space. The design looks beautiful, and we'll see it better when the model is finished next week. But my job is to advise my clients when I think their plans may be off. The design of these buildings will cost you a fortune every year, starting on the day the buildings open for business."

"I know, I know, but don't you worry, lass. Old Angus can afford it."

"But by chopping off the second and third floors, you're giving up 90,000 square of retail space, at an average net loss of $3.6 million a year, just on the first five projects. You're the boss, but my job is to give you the facts, not just design buildings."

He let out a deep breath. I didn't sense that he was annoyed with me, even though he had every right to be. I was being a pain in the ass, and I knew it. But an architect's job often entails keeping a client out of trouble. He looked almost resigned, as if he agreed with my objection. I had the impression that he seemed to be going along with an idea he disagreed with, almost as if someone else was pulling the strings.

"Do you think we'll hit our target date of the day after Thanksgiving next year, Ellen?"

"Yes, I do. Of course the work schedule is for the construction supervisors, but I've seen large projects done in less time. The plans are almost complete. If I may offer my opinion, Angus, I think your idea of opening the day after Thanksgiving is brilliant. Black Friday, the day that a retailer's bottom line changes from red to black, is the busiest shopping day of the year. That's not the opinion of an architect, but the business woman in me thinks it's a great strategy."

"Yes, I suppose. There will be thousands of shoppers in the centers looking for bargains. Thousands."

As he said that, I again had the feeling that he wasn't happy about it. This was freaking me out. I'd think that a huge successful opening would make him excited. But he seemed almost sad. Maybe I was getting like Rick, suspicious about everything, but this man looked forlorn about something.

"So I'll meet you in your office next Tuesday to see the model, lassie."

As I gathered up the plans and slipped them into the carrying case, I had to ask a question.

"Tell me, Angus, if you don't mind my asking. Your assistant has a charming accent, but I just can't place it. Where is she from?"

"Oh, I don't know. Somewhere in the Middle East, I think."

CHAPTER EIGHT

I woke up this morning feeling like shit. Ellen had just put a cup of tea next to my side of the bed. It's hard to describe, but we all know the feeling of a cold coming on. Fortunately, I don't get a lot of colds. I take my vitamins, get exercise and rest, and generally take care of myself. But a cold virus doesn't give a rat's ass how much you take care of yourself. The little bugger could be lurking on a door handle or a handrail.

Ellen tells me I get cranky when I have cold. She's right. When I have cold, I feel like something is blocking me from getting my work done. My muddled head doesn't help much either. I constantly blow my nose and wipe my eyes.

I just have to stop whining and get to work. I took my daytime cold medicine. It helped a little, at least in the runny nose department. But with all of the mayhem engulfing the counterterrorism task force, I didn't have the luxury of staying in bed. I'll just keep drinking liquids and hang in there. Ellen can switch from lover to kindly grandmother in an instant. That morning she tried to get me to stay home, but she knew that wouldn't happen. Then she tried to convince me to go to the doctor. I'm not afraid of doctors, but the simple truth was there is no cure for the common cold. Just treat the symptoms, which I was trying to do.

⤙⤚

Buster, Dr. Bennie, my partner Zeke, and I sat down around the conference table in my office for the first of our many meetings. Not wanting to share my germs, I insisted on sitting down at the end of the table. I brought a box of antiseptic hand wipes to keep the surfaces I touched bug free. Zeke ordered a tray of sandwiches because he knew the meeting would be long. Bennie knew about my cold because we had spoken earlier on the phone. He brought a quart-sized container of chicken soup, which he made himself.

"God bless you," they all said in response to my latest sneeze.

It was Thursday, November 13, almost a month since the attacks of 10/15. If there's one thing I hate, it's being up against a case when I have no clue how to proceed. I felt good about having this meeting, except for my goddamn cold. My colleagues are sharp, and by the end of the meeting we hoped to have some direction. At least that was my plan.

"Buster, I'd like you to start the meeting," I said as I blew my nose. "You have a reputation as a guy who likes to get things done."

"You haven't heard the least of it, Rick," said Bennie. "We joke that Buster is a human action figure. I've seen him pull off some of the weirdest shit that you can imagine."

"Thanks for the confidence, Bennie. You're both right. I like to get results."

Buster stood and carried a flip chart from the corner of my office closer to the table. He turned the chart so we could see it.

"Here's where we are, and here's what we know," said Buster. "The enemy we face isn't the enemy we're used to. The enemy could be the guy next door. It's easy to keep track of Arabs because they look like me. But these killers aren't Arabs, although they all have something in common. Anybody want to take a stab at what that is?"

"They're all 'homegrown' terrorists," I said. "They all converted to Islam."

"And their psychological profile," said Bennie, "is that they have personality disorders. Some of them are borderline psychopaths, from the little we know about them."

"None of them have Middle Eastern backgrounds," said Zeke.

"But there is something else they have in common," said Buster, "something that precedes the excellent observations you guys just made. There's something about them that's traceable and trackable. We have the ability to narrow down the group and possibly even predict their behavior."

"Holy shit," said Ben. "You've come up with a way to get to them before they detonate the next bomb?"

"I second Bennie's 'holy shit,' " I said.

"Third," said Zeke.

Buster smiled. He smiled like a guy who just got the response he was looking for.

"Okay, guys, here it is. You all have Top Secret security clearances, and most important, you have a need to know. I don't have to explain that to you. You're pros, and you're about to hear the most Top Secret project in the CIA. What all of the attackers of 10/15 have in common is that they posted comments on various sites on the Internet. Some were even dumb enough to post under their own usernames on Facebook and Twitter. Once a person goes public on the Internet, they're fair game. We don't need warrants to check what's public. So once we've identified a person as a radical, we still can't get a warrant unless we can show intent to commit an illegal act. But those signs are all over the place. One of the attackers had a phone conversation in which he said he was 'ready to use the sword of Allah on 10/15.' "

"But how did you tap the guy's phone?" I asked, wiping my nose on a tissue. "He's dead. How did you get a warrant?"

"We convinced the Foreign Intelligence Surveillance Court, better known as the FISA Court, to give us warrants on all of the attackers of 10/15. We argued in court that because we could seize assets if the person was found to have done the act, that property interest alone was enough to trigger a warrant, even though the 'suspects' were all dead."

"You must have some persuasive lawyers," Zeke said.

"For the 10/15 warrants," said Buster, "we hired some of the best constitutional lawyers in the country. The 10/15 warrants were that important. But here's the most important thing. Because we had detailed information on all of the 10/15 killers, we were able to plug that data into our computers. We ran it through an amazing algorithm and came up with more dots and more patterns than you can believe. In a strange way, the attacks of 10/15 gave us the tools to look into the future and try to prevent the next attack, using the profiles shown by the algorithm. We now have a mother lode of profile data from 12 actual killers."

"Wait a minute," I said. "All of this assumes that a potential suicide bomber first gets onto a website and posts something. What if some smart jihadi figures this all out and just makes sure he stays away from the Internet?"

"That's unlikely," said Bennie. "A suicide bomber, remember, has to show the world his miserable life meant something. That's why so many of them make videos of themselves before they act. And also, don't assume that these jihadis are all that smart. Their paranoid delusions usually control their behavior."

"But I'm still not getting something," I said. "So we find a suspect by tracking his public Internet activity, and then we convince the FISA court to give us a warrant. We search all of the allowable records, including phone calls, and come up with nothing more than a suspicion. How do we nail the guy before he acts?"

"Great point, Rick," said Buster. "The simple answer is that, as Bennie said, we know from the profile that the suspect is likely to show some signs before he acts. But the bottom line is this: it will cut down on the vast number of suspects. Only a jihadi with as much smarts and training as the four of us will get through the screening. Of all the killers on 10/15, we could have ID'd every one of them if we knew then what we know now. The job won't be simple. It will entail a lot of basic police work. Once we find a bad guy who's planning something, we tail him and put surveillance devices on his car, all of which we're allowed to do with a FISA court warrant."

"It seems to me that this is both good news and bad news," I said. "It gives me the creeps to know that we can find so much about an American citizen without his knowledge."

"Rick, these FISA Court judges are no pushovers. We really have to present compelling evidence to get a warrant. And the Senate Intelligence Committee is all over this process. Nobody wants the FBI or CIA to turn into the Gestapo. But the good news is that we now have the best means we've ever had to prevent terrorist attacks."

"So what's going on now, with all of this new technology and a bunch of profiles?" asked Bennie.

"I have a team of seven agents who do nothing but monitor the extremist websites, using the software I told you about. They also monitor social media sites like Twitter for interesting hashtags, like *#jihad*, or *#deathtoamerica*. Once the algorithm starts blinking red lights, we then go to the FISA court for a warrant."

"What about mosques and Islamic schools? Not everything in the world gets done on the Internet," said Bennie.

"Bennie, let me say this. You don't have a need to know about that at this point. To be clear, you don't *want* to fucking know. Just rest assured that we're not stupid—and neither is the FBI."

Bennie looked at me. I just closed my eyes and nodded.

"So we find a suspect, get a FISA court warrant, do surveillance, and nab him," said Bennie. "You guys are the lawyers, but I know damn well that to get a conviction, we have to prove guilt of a crime beyond a reasonable doubt. That can be a tall order as you know. What if the bad guy gets acquitted or the judge throws out the case for lack of evidence? Then what do we do with the guy?"

"Don't go there my friend," said Buster. "Don't go there."

CHAPTER NINE

"Buster," I said, "this bothers me. We're able to eavesdrop on anybody who happens to look at a radical website. There could be innocent reasons. Hell, what about your CIA team? They're constantly on the different sites. And what about people who are just curious, or a journalist doing research for an article?"

"You're right, Rick. Just because somebody visits a radical website doesn't mean he's a potential terrorist. Our algorithm accounts for those circumstances. Let's take a look at one guy who seems to have been living on these sites for the past couple of months. This man visits each of the websites at least five times a day, and he spends a lot of time on each site. Sounds suspicious? Now take a look at this. The man is a writer, and here's an article that was published over his name in *The Atlantic*. As you can see, it's a feature-length article that discusses the content of each of the radical sites. He goes into detail and also wrote about the content of the posts themselves. So he's just a writer, and a damn good one. I'm including his stuff in our research materials. Nothing wrong with the guy. He's just a journalist and researcher. I don't doubt that as we drill down further, we'll find all sorts of politicians, not to mention law enforcement people, showing up on these sites. No, don't worry Rick. We're not dumb enough to assume that a radical site visit, in itself, is any kind of a red flag. Our algorithm doesn't work that way either because it tracks other posts from the website site visitor. When it sees that he's written about what he's researched, it doesn't flag him as a potential bad guy. Yes, it's creepy, but that's why we have oversight, people like the Senate Intelligence Committee. I know we look like Big Brother, but we're a law-abiding Big Brother."

"Why don't we talk about some of the people your algorithm flagged as suspects?" asked Zeke. "Why don't we look at somebody we may want to talk to?"

"Okay," said Buster, "let's look at a man that our algorithm blew a circuit over, a guy who is a blinking red light. Actually, the guy is a gal named Denise McLaren. A few years ago, our profiling would eliminate females, but welcome to the new world of radical jihad. I remind you that five of the twelve bombers of 10/15 were women."

"Did you get a FISA court warrant to check her further?" asked Bennie.

"Yes, we did. And you're about to see why. Ms. McLaren is 23 years old and graduated from the University of Wisconsin with a degree in sociology. As of a year ago, she worked for a group called People of Peace, which is associated with CAIR, the Council on American-Islamic Relations. They're mainly a bunch of researchers who feed data and information to CAIR for its propaganda. Sorry I meant to say *educational outreach*. Her phone records show that she talks to a source in Yemen at least once a week. The source was tracked to a man on our terror watch list. She's posted about a dozen messages on the radical sites, including this one: 'I will soon explode for the love of Allah.' We've put a tracking device on her car, and a member of my team monitors her movements constantly. We also have an agent who personally follows her."

"Buster," said Dr. Bennie, "do you have any idea why this young woman has turned to radical Islam? Is there anything in her past to give a hint why she's become disaffected with her culture?"

"Well, Bennie, you're probably the best one in the room to answer that question. Let me explain what we know about her background. In her junior year at Wisconsin, she filed a sexual harassment complaint against a fellow student. She claimed date rape. As you know, universities take these complaints seriously. But her complaint was dismissed in about a month, along with a rebuke against her for having filed it. It seems that the guy she complained about had an ironclad alibi. He was out of the country at the time of the alleged incident. Then she followed up with another complaint against a different student in her senior year. Same result, and another rebuke, with a warning of expulsion. Further investigation showed that she dated each of the complaint targets briefly, but both guys called off the relationship. From interviews with some of the students, our operatives concluded that this was a simple case of a girl being jilted, twice in a year. In her final semester she almost flunked out. She took to Facebook to air her feelings about her two complaints. It seems that her fellow students, both men and women, were pissed off at her, and they all took the side of the complaint targets. Those postings against her could best be described as ridicule."

"So," said Dr. Bennie, "I'm picking up a strong whiff of embarrassment, a strong feeling of 'why's everybody always picking on me?' As trivial as it may sound, feelings of shame and embarrassment often lead to revenge, either in the form of blackmail or in some cases violence. Her personal life was coming apart, and she had a couple of scores to settle. We could theorize that her turn to radicalism was a complicated way to retrieve her sense of worth, a self-imposed culture of 'her against the infidels.' How many times have we read about a loner who strikes out with violence because his or her personal life took a bad turn? Suicides are often the result of this kind of screwed up personal life. But when you combine suicide with an allegiance to a cause, and a chance to take down a lot of other people with you, you begin to see a pattern."

"Bennie," said Zeke, "are you saying that these acts of horrible violence could be the result of jilted love affairs or some kind of other public embarrassment?"

"Yes, Zeke, that's exactly what I'm saying. The human mind can be a strange thing, take it from me. I won't suggest that we'll always see this pattern, but it's a strong indicator. How else do you explain a modern young American suddenly adopting a bizarre ideology from the Dark Ages? It's less a case of converting to a cause than of finding something to hold onto, an alternative, a sharp turn in the opposite direction. It's a way to give a meaningless life some meaning."

⇒⊹ ⊹⇐

"It's been about a month since the attacks," said Buster. "So far they've targeted transportation and office buildings. We need to think about how else can they hurt the infidels, their perceived enemy?"

"Do you think another round of attacks will happen soon?" I asked.

"I have a gut feeling that things will calm down for a while," said Buster. "The enemy knows that we're on hyper-alert. They know that our guard is up."

None of us said anything. We just looked at Buster.

"But I could be wrong."

CHAPTER TEN

At 7:30 on the morning of November 14, the *Ocean Mariner,* an American flagged cruise ship, steamed through the Narrows, the body of water at the entrance to New York Harbor. Its destination was Port Liberty in Bayonne, New Jersey, a cruise line terminal owned by Royal Caribbean. Security on the ship, as well as on every cruise ship in the world, was at its highest because of the attacks of 10/15.

A terrorist attack on a cruise ship hadn't happened in a long time. In 1985, terrorists took over the ship *Achille Lauro* off the coast of Egypt. After they were denied permission to dock the ship in Syria, the hijackers shot Leon Klinghoffer to death. He was a disabled American Jewish businessman, confined to a wheelchair. After they shot him, the terrorists dumped his body into the ocean. That was 30 years ago.

⊶ ⊷

The pilot boat pulled alongside the *Ocean Mariner* so that the harbor pilot could board the ship. This was a standard practice for any ship entering a large port. The pilot, as he is called, is an expert in the local waters, a sort of valet parker to make sure the ship arrives safely in port.

The captain of the pilot boat expertly maneuvered his vessel next to the ship. As the boat tied up to the platform on the starboard side of the *Ocean Mariner*, a bomb detonated. The gigantic blast ripped through the hull of the cruise ship, destroying all starboard side cabins to a height of 100 feet. It also ripped a gaping hole below the waterline. Blast debris and body parts rained down on the nearby Belt Parkway, causing 30 serious car accidents, some fatal.

With water gushing through its decks, the *Ocean Mariner* took a steep list and rolled over onto its starboard side within 10 minutes. The assembly areas on the first deck were flooded instantly, drowning hundreds of vacationers who were waiting in lounge areas for their disembarkation instructions. Because the water was shallow, a large part of the *Ocean Mariner* protruded from the harbor. The ship was about 1,000 feet from the Verrazano-Narrows Bridge, giving morning commuters a spectacle of pure horror.

"Okay, people, let's look at what we've got," I said. I was feeling like my old self now that my cold was just about gone.

I had to fight back the urge to throw up, and it had nothing to do with my departing cold. I arrived at the office early that day, and so did Buster, Bennie, and Zeke. We got news of the *Ocean Mariner* about 10 minutes after we arrived. I'd noticed something about myself. Anytime I clicked on a news channel, I had a feeling like I just put my hand into a hornet's nest.

Buster was on the phone, taking notes. He hung up and walked over to the flip chart.

"I just got off the phone with the Sandy Hook Pilots Association. I spoke to a guy who tossed off the lines to the pilot boat before it left the pier to meet the ship. He said the only people aboard were the normal crew of four, including the pilot. So from what we know right now, the pilot

boat wasn't hijacked. The guy I spoke to said there is a crewmember who sleeps aboard the boat every night."

"Did you get the names of the crew?" Bennie asked.

Buster looked at him as if he was insane.

"Of *course* I got the names. They're already being fed into the computer at the CIA."

I had heard that Buster was usually 10 steps ahead of everyone else, and I just saw confirmation of that.

Buster sat in front of a computer terminal and checked his encrypted email messages. He had gotten off the phone only 10 minutes earlier, but already the information was pouring in. As an FBI guy, I had to say these CIA spooks were impressive – and fast.

"Okay, here's what we got," said Buster. "Nobody was on any sort of a watch list, and our algorithm never beeped a word about any of them."

"But you just fed those names in," I said. "How can we get the information so fast?"

"Harbor pilots are a group of people we've checked out in advance. It's a no-brainer that they could potentially cause mayhem. So all the computer had to do was update the information on the names."

"And here's something," said Zeke. "That was one big fucking bomb. I just read on the online edition of *The New York Times* that one expert says it had the size and explosive power of the Oklahoma City bomb that almost took down the Murrah Federal building."

"Can anybody explain to me how a boatload of good guys can manage to deliver a bomb without realizing it?" asked Buster.

"With all due respect to your computer algorithm, Buster" said Bennie, "I think that we're going to find something we may have missed, something that hadn't been fed into the computer that may implicate one of these guys. The guy you spoke to said that the boat was manned 24/7. Nobody could sneak a large bomb aboard without the watchman noticing."

"Let's pay a visit to the guy who sleeps on the boat," I said.

Bennie, Buster, Zeke, and I went to the Sandy Hook Pilots Association building on Edgewater Street on the New York City Borough of Staten Island. The building was one story and covered with stucco, nestled by the Narrows.

Thank God my cold was almost gone and I could breathe in the fresh air. The weather was mild for mid-November, about 60 degrees. It felt good.

Mike Simonetti, the man who slept on the pilot boat the night before, was waiting for us in a small office. I introduced everyone and we sat around a small table. The room had a large window facing the water, covered with cracks from the explosion's blast wave. We could see the hulk of the *Ocean Mariner* lying on its side in about 50 feet of water, less than a quarter mile from our location.

"Is it okay if we call you Mike?" I asked.

"Sure," said Simonetti. "We're an informal group."

"Mike, before we begin, I have to ask you something. Are you feeling okay?"

"No, I'm not. I just got back from Staten Island University Hospital. When the crew reported to the boat this morning, I was fast asleep, but the problem was they couldn't wake me up. An EMT told me that they had to physically carry me off the boat and load me into the ambulance. I'm still a little groggy, and I feel like shit. I lost three good friends this morning."

"Did the doctor say what was wrong with you?"

"No, but they took a blood test and let me go after I seemed better."

Buster excused himself and went outside to make a phone call.

"Why do you guys assign someone to sleep on the boat?" Zeke asked. "Security?"

"It's a little extra security. Those pilot boats have a lot of expensive equipment. But the main reason we keep a guy on the boat is to start the engines in case we get an emergency assignment to meet a ship. The guy on the boat turns on the ignition and it's ready to go when the pilot comes aboard."

"Are you a pilot?"

"I'm in training. I hope to have my license by next year."

"Did you have any alcohol last night?" I asked.

"Not a drop. The whole idea behind having a guy aboard is to get underway fast if we have to. Booze and alertness don't go together."

Buster came back into the room.

"It's no wonder you're groggy," said Buster. "According to the hospital, you had enough sleeping medication to drug an elephant."

"But how the hell could I have taken it? I never use sleeping pills."

"Do you carry a thermos or any other liquids with you?"

"I always carry a thermos filled with tea."

"Tell us more about the thermos. Did you leave it anywhere before you boarded the boat, where somebody may have slipped you a good night dose?"

"Let me think. Yes, I left the thermos in the kitchen here in the building after I filled it with tea, while I went back to my car to get my Kindle. I like to read at night."

"Was anybody here who you didn't recognize?"

"Yes, a guy who said he was from the Coast Guard walked into the building at around 5:30. He said he was here to drop off some paperwork. I thought it was weird because he wasn't wearing a uniform. He was in the building while I went to my car."

"Did he give you his name? Can you describe him?"

"He didn't tell me his name, and I had no reason to ask him. He was white, about six feet tall, skinny, with sandy blond hair."

"Anything else about this man that you can tell us?"

"He had a slight accent, Irish or English, I think. He sounded a bit like John Lennon. A cockney accent, like he was from Liverpool."

"Was anybody else in the building while he was here?"

"No, it was empty, except for him. I guess it was dumb of me to leave him here alone, but we don't think too much about security around here. We have a private security guard who walks around occasionally."

"I want that kitchen secured as of right now," I said. "Zeke, please grab some crime scene tape from the car. I want the kitchen dusted for prints."

"Did you see the security guard before you got on the boat?" I asked.

"No, I didn't see him."

My cell phone buzzed. It was a message from headquarters.

"I just found out why you didn't see the security guard last night. He was shot through the head in his guard shack."

"Mike," said Buster, "thank you for your help. We'll probably have more questions for you during this investigation, so check your phone for messages. Go home and get some sleep."

"Okay, guys," I said, "I think we should have a close-up look at the ship. I've arranged for a Coast Guard patrol boat to pick us up at the pier in 10 minutes. Maybe a Coastie can tell us if he

⊰┼┼⊱

As we stood by the pier waiting for the Coast Guard boat, we discussed our interview with Simonetti.

"So, Dr. Bullshit Detector," I said to Bennie, "what's your take on Mike Simonetti?"

"The guy was telling the truth, Rick. Not one indication of bullshit. I look for about a dozen signs to see if a person is lying, including eye movements, perspiration, hand movements, and stuff like that. He could have made up a story why he left an unidentified stranger alone in the building, which was a real fuck-up on his part, but he didn't. The guy's for real."

"He also gave us a good description of the skinny blond guy with the cockney accent," I said. "After we get the fingerprint results back, we should have a lead," said Buster. "All of the people who work for the pilots association are fingerprinted and the records are kept by the Coast Guard."

"Any chance of plugging in blond hair, slight build, and cockney accent into your algorithm, Buster?" asked Zeke with a chuckle.

"Already did it. So far my guys have narrowed it down to four people. Hey, when I said we work fast, I wasn't kidding. As soon as we get some photographs of the possible targets we'll pass them by Simonetti."

"Buster, you amaze me," I said.

"Thanks, Rick. I'm just a spook on a case."

"What's wrong with the picture so far?" I asked. "Is there anything that stands out?"

"Yes," said Zeke. "We always seem to be closing the barn door after the horse got out. So here we are at a pier where boats leave to meet large ships. And all they had was one security guard. They didn't even think to install security cameras on the building, like any grocery store owner would. Every time something explodes, we always say, gee, we should have thought about that. And this is almost a month after 10/15."

"Here comes the boat," I said. "Zeke's right. We have to start thinking about what we should do *before* shit happens."

⟛⟛

The Coast Guard patrol boat maneuvered slowly around the hulk of the *Ocean Mariner*. Because the water was only 50 feet deep and the ship's beam was 154 feet, more than two-thirds of the vessel could be seen from shore. Commuters on the Belt Parkway and the Verrazano Bridge would be treated to a sickening view for months.

The bomb-equipped pilot boat exploded on the starboard side of the ship, which now rested on the bottom. All we could see was part of the ship. The divers with cameras would find out a lot more than we could possibly see from the surface of the water.

"Let's get out of here," I said. "We're wasting our time until we have some evidence from the divers."

"Wait!" Buster yelled. "Hey captain, pull the boat up next to that debris off to the starboard side."

A plastic sign, about two feet by four feet floated on the surface. I grabbed a boat hook and pulled it next to us. Zeke reached down and hoisted it aboard. The sign read, "MacPherson International."

CHAPTER TWELVE

"May peace be with you, brother Bashara," said Greg Nolan with his British cockney accent.

The two men met at a secluded vacant house in Perth Amboy, New Jersey. Bashara sat behind an old desk and Nolan sat in a chair facing him.

"I will call you by your infidel name, Greg Nolan, as we are all disciplining ourselves to do. I would prefer to call you Muhammad Chudri, but the rules have changed. You have executed our plans for the cruise ship perfectly, Greg. I commend you on a job well done. You efficiently killed the watchman with a silencer, and you supervised the bomb-loading crew with a calmness that made it all possible."

"I thank you sir. It was my privilege to be part of such a glorious mission."

"Perhaps the best part of the outcome is that it will take months before the ship can be righted and moved. Months of showing the commuting heathens on the bridge and the parkway the justice of Allah. As foreign vessels pull into the harbor, there will be photographs sent all over the world, showing all nations how we execute our plans."

"It was my pleasure, Ali, I mean Phil. I sat in my car by the Verrazano Bridge and watched with pleasure as thousands of infidels were sent to hell. It is a memory that will never leave me, a constant reminder of our glorious mission."

"And it is a memory that you deserve to relish, Greg."

"It was the greatest assignment you have given me to date. I await your orders for my next task. I vow that I will execute it with the same care I used for the cruise ship operation. Do you have one prepared for me now?"

Bashara raised a Colt 45 automatic pistol and fired it at Nolan's head, killing him instantly.

"May peace be with you, brother Greg."

CHAPTER THIRTEEN

I t was 8 p.m. and I had just arrived home. Ellen and I had a habit of eating a light supper, a good way to keep our weight under control, and also a good way to handle the schedule of a compulsive FBI agent. As always, Ellen met me at the door and gave me a hug, not just a "Hi, how are you hug," but a hug that says, "I love you."

Ellen knows there's a lot about my work that I can't share with her. It isn't a matter of trust – it's just sound policy. She understands the "need to know" rule. Even if a person is entirely trustworthy, and that describes Ellen, it's a bad practice to divulge information that she may inadvertently blurt out. The old World War II saying, "loose lips sink ships," couldn't be more accurate.

And Ellen gets it. Even though she's smart as hell and would love to know everything about what's going on, she understands.

"So how was your day, hon?" she asked.

We both cracked up at her subtle joke. There was a lot about today that I couldn't tell her, but I'd be damned if I said, "I can't talk about it." I decided to tell her all about it, minus the open investigative details.

"And how's your cold?"

"Finally gone. I'm all better, thanks in no small part to your constant administration of chicken soup."

After a day of sweaty armpits and saltwater spray, I needed to rinse off.

After my shower, we sat in the living room with me in my terry robe. There's something about the feeling of terrycloth that is very calming.

"I'm feeling punchy, Ellen. We all thought that after 10/15, things would calm down, but we're one sunken cruise ship beyond that hope. I guess you've been watching the news reports."

"It's impossible not to hear about it if you turn on the TV. Do you want me to put it on, hon?"

"No, I've seen enough horror today. I'd like to spend some quiet time with the lady I love." We kissed.

"Well, here's the consensus of opinion of all of the network and cable anchors," she said. "It was a terrorist bombing, using a bomb planted in a harbor pilot boat. A few hours ago, they stopped saying that 'terrorism can't be ruled out.' They talked about a security guard who was shot and killed. The press is now calling it an act of terror."

"And they're right. I spent most of the day at the Sandy Hook Pilots Association on Staten Island. Obviously I can't go into a lot of detail, but this was a sophisticated terror gig, much more sophisticated than the attacks of 10/15."

"There's so goddamn much that we don't know about, hon," Ellen said. "I can tell from the look on your face that you're trying to think ahead."

"What really freaks me out, babe, are the things that are not even on my mind. Things that I don't know that I don't know."

And I had an ugly feeling that I was about to find out some of those things soon.

CHAPTER FOURTEEN

"May peace be with you, brother Ali," said Joe Portman as he walked into Ali Bashara's apartment in Jersey City. Portman, disguised as a woman, wore a full burqa, covering his body as well as his head and face.

"And may peace be with you, brother Joe."

"Please, Ali, call me by my Muslim name, Abbas Muktada."

"No, brother Joe. Your name is one of the reasons for our meeting today. You are Joseph Portman. You were born with that name, and I want you to forget the name Abbas Muktada. Am I making myself clear, Joseph Portman?"

"But Ali, ever since I embraced Islam three years ago, I have loved my new name, a name that gives praise to Allah. Now you're telling me I must revert to my infidel name, a name of darkness?"

"You know who I am, Joe, yes? Tell me what you know about my background so I can be sure."

"You're a 37-year-old computer scientist, and until two years ago you were a manager with Google. You graduated from MIT with a bachelor's degree in math and a doctorate in computer science.

Until you converted to Islam, I believe 10 years ago, your heathen name was Phillip Murphy."

"So you agree that I know what I'm talking about when the subject is computers?"

"Of course, Ali, you're the smartest technologist I know."

"Call me Phil, not Ali. My name is Phillip Murphy."

"You baffle me. Why are we adopting the names of infidels? Are we not worshippers of Allah and followers of his prophet Muhammad, peace be upon him?"

"Yes, we are, Joe, and that's why we will no longer use our Muslim names."

"Please explain…Phil."

"You've just said that you trust my knowledge of computer science. I believe you said that I'm the smartest technologist you know, and thank you for the compliment. So listen to what I am about to tell you, and keep it in your mind, never to be divulged. Agreed?"

"Of course."

"I, along with some of my computer scientist brothers, have learned that the infidels have come up with a powerful computer algorithm to identify jihadis, especially American-born jihadis like you and me. We've been studying their activities for months, and we have concluded that we must take action. Do you understand what I mean by an algorithm, Joe?"

"Yes, it's a formula or a procedure for calculating complicated pieces of data. It's how Google can figure out what websites to recommend to us, based on what we put into a search term."

"You have a good basic understanding of what I'm about to explain. If a researcher feeds enough relevant information into a database, an algorithm can show the investigator what he's looking for. The more data, the more accurate the result. So let me bring this into focus as it applies to us. As you know, both of us, and hundreds of other faithful American Muslims are being called 'homegrown radicals,' meaning that we're not from a foreign country but born Americans, part of American culture. This 'homegrown' process, here and across the world, is developing into our single best means for defeating the infidels, the single best way to advance the goal of a caliphate on earth. Look at the glorious success of October 15. We could not have done that with a bunch of Middle Eastern-looking people with names like Ali. Every one of the martyrs looked as American as you and me."

"But what does this have to do with a computer algorithm?" asked Portman.

"We want to choke off its supply of data. No data, no knowledge. And if they have no knowledge we're free to act on our plans. And we will cut off the data by acting in every way like infidel Americans. No Facebook or Twitter postings in praise of Islam. No surfing around radical websites. And absolutely no use of our Muslim names. When we are rewarded in heaven, Allah will sing our praise in our proper names, and the virgins will whisper them into our ears."

"And what will be my role, Phil?"

"What I am about to tell you, Joe, will blow your mind."

"Phil, you *are* blowing my fucking mind. Oh, praise to Allah, I haven't spoken with such heathen vulgarity in years."

"That's perfectly okay, Joe. That's the way a typical American would speak, and it's our job to look, act, and talk like typical Americans. Fuckin A, babe," said Murphy as he gave Portman a high five.

"And here's how we're going to do this, Joe. First, I know that you have spent a lot of time on jihadi websites. You will stop that immediately. I believe the CIA algorithm probably knows about your activity over the years, so I'm giving you this article I wrote. I want you to copy it and post it over your name, Joseph Portman, on an Internet writing site like HubPages. As you can see in the article, you discuss your visits to the websites. You are writing as an amateur journalist. The article in no way says anything positive about Islam, just a review of the different sites. This will create a new profile for you, a profile that gives an innocent explanation why you visited those sites. The algorithm will exclude you as a person of interest.

"Next, you will not set foot in a mosque. You have a prayer rug, I'm sure. Use it to worship in your own home. I know you've been careful when visiting mosques by disguising yourself, but your visits must stop. Then, I want you to shave off your beard. And never wear a taqiyah. The only head covering you will ever wear will be a baseball cap or a stocking hat for winter.

"Further, you and I will not communicate by email or phone. The only way to contact me is by Twitter. I have a list of code phrases that we will use. When you tweet, you will not send me a DM or direct message, nor will you send me a tweet. You will simply post it in your timeline at specified times of the day, and I will check for your message at those times. I don't want the risk that the CIA or FBI is monitoring my keystrokes, which I'm sure they're doing. They have some brilliant programmers, as I found out when I worked for Google."

"What if I need to contact you immediately, Phil?"

"You will text to one of a dozen phone numbers at random. I'll give you the numbers shortly. Each of the brothers with the numbers will know to immediately send me a coded text to contact you. I will do so via Twitter. You'll have to monitor your Twitter timeline carefully if you ever have to use this procedure."

"But, Phil, what about our American brothers who haven't been as careful as me about keeping their Muslim identities confidential?"

"Each of them will soon be visited by me or one of my colleagues from al-Qaeda. They will be told the same information that I'm giving you today. Some of them have been so publicly vocal about their religion that their use as jihadis has been totally compromised."

"I feel like I'm in shock, Phil. Since I embraced Islam a few years ago, I've had the urge to 'spread the word.' Now you're telling me that the only part of my faith I can practice is on a prayer rug in my apartment."

"That's right. We will praise Allah and bring him glory by becoming, at least outwardly, people we would rather not be. We will live in the shadows. Is everything I said clear to you?"

"Perfectly clear, Phil."

⚊╫ ╫⚊

"Good morning, ladies and gentlemen, I'm Shepard Smith reporting for Fox News. What I have to tell you this morning is upsetting to say the least. I'm going to talk about a number and how that number fits into our history.

"Tallying up the building lobby attacks, the bombings of commuter railroads on 10/15, and the sinking of the *Ocean Mariner* on November 14, the death toll now stands at 3,115. This is higher than the number of deaths from the attacks of 9/11, and, of course, higher than the deaths at Pearl Harbor. And, because 75 people are still in critical condition, the number could get larger.

"The questions on everyone's mind are the same: When will the attacks ever stop? Has 10/15 signaled the beginning of a new era in history? Will there ever be a time when we can turn on the radio or TV and not have a sickening feeling in our stomachs?

"The enemy has changed. The enemy looks just like the rest of us, doesn't talk with an accent, and doesn't appear to be foreign. The enemy consists of native born Americans, Americans who have sworn allegiance to a perversion of a religion, an enemy that wants to kill, and kill in large numbers.

"My job isn't to alarm people, but as a journalist I have to report the facts. Those facts are alarming. America is under siege.

The last thing we want is panic, but another thing none of us wants is complacency.

"We've been told for years, 'If you see something, say something.' That advice has never been more urgent. When the enemy doesn't wear a uniform and looks and sounds like the guy or gal next door, we all have a duty to help.

In other news…"

CHAPTER FIFTEEN

On the afternoon of November 20, *The Sovereign of the Deep*, a 950-foot, 90,000-ton cruise ship owned and operated by Cunard, cast off its lines and steamed majestically down the Grand Canal in Venice, Italy. After the attack and sinking of the *Ocean Mariner* in New York only a week before, security was almost military in its thoroughness. The pilot boat hired by Cunard was checked so closely it could have been a medical procedure.

Armed vessels of the Italian Coast Guard were stationed all along the Grand Canal. Armored vehicles rolled along the streets near the canal. Soldiers, armed with Uzi submachine guns, patrolled the upper decks of the ship. They also carried rocket-propelled grenade guns in case a menacing vessel approached.

Although the sinking of the *Ocean Mariner* happened so recently, surprisingly few travelers canceled their cruise on *The Sovereign of the Deep*. People interviewed by journalists all reported the same basic feeling. "A cruise ship sinking? That's not likely to happen again soon."

━┿━ ━┿━

A medium-size jet, an Airbus A318, took off from Venice Airport, headed for Turin. There, it would pick up 100 passengers, all employees of Fiat, the Italian car manufacturer, for a charter flight to New York. The captain topped off the fuel tanks in Venice before departing. As the plane left Venice, only six crew members were aboard, four Italians, including the pilot, co-pilot and two assistants, an American navigator, and a German flight engineer.

As the plane gained altitude, the pilot, Giuseppe Aldonzo, could see the cruise ship below about three miles into the Adriatic after departing Venice. He banked the plane away from the ship, then turned and descended.

Alfredo Manzani, captain of *The Sovereign of the Deep*, stepped out onto the starboard wing of the bridge to observe a crew drill being conducted on the foredeck. In the final moments of his life, he looked up and saw the Airbus flying straight for the bridge.

The explosion was bomb-like because the plane's fuel tanks were filled to capacity. The plane ripped into the ship's bridge, and the firestorm exploded aft, engulfing three of the ship's restaurants, passenger cabins on both sides, and every deck from the highest down to the waterline. The plane hit so suddenly, there wasn't enough time to send out a distress alarm. No other vessels were within view of the ship.

The Sovereign of the Deep, now a crippled hulk of fire and smoke, began a slow list to the starboard side. After 25 minutes, it capsized and sank in 300 feet of water.

Michael Johanssen, the Canadian captain of the freighter *Prince*, heard the explosion and saw smoke over the horizon. He steered his ship toward the smoke, alerting the Italian Coast Guard as he did. In a half hour, the *Prince* steamed through a large debris field. Although his ship was in danger, Johanssen was a seasoned mariner and the code of the sea was in his blood. He'd be damned if he wouldn't do everything possible to look for survivors. As the *Prince* steamed slowly through the debris field, Johanssen realized that the likelihood of finding any survivors was low.

Three large cutters from the Italian Coast Guard soon joined *Prince* in the search. The pounding thuds of helicopter rotors filled the air. None of the 2,500 passengers or 842 crewmembers survived.

CHAPTER SIXTEEN

Ellen and I had lunch in a small cafe off Houston Street. I didn't have much of an appetite, having watched the news about the attack on the cruise ship off the coast of Italy. No one survived.

Interpol had been in touch with Buster and the CIA to try to piece it all together. I wondered about the chances of finding the plane's cockpit data recorder, the black box, in 300 feet of water after a gigantic explosion. Without witnesses, the only hope of finding out what happened was the black box. Buster was doing a background check on the six crewmembers of the plane.

"Our workout this morning felt good," I said. "We both needed it."

"Our workout last night was even better," said Ellen with a wry smile.

I reached over and stroked her face.

"Without you, I don't know how I could put up with all this crap. You're my connection to sanity."

"Hey, Rick, you look upset. What's the matter, hon?"

"Aren't *you* upset?"

"Oh yeah, that cruise ship in Italy. Horrible. So yes, I'm upset too. I guess your algorithm didn't pick up any signals about the crew of the Italian jet."

"What algorithm? I didn't tell you anything about an algorithm."

"Rick, you spend almost every working hour connecting dots, looking for patterns. To me it's obvious that you or the CIA has a computer algorithm that analyzes your data. I'm sure you guys don't keep track of terrorists by scribbling notes on the back of napkins. It's obvious, at least to me, that you have a structured way of keeping track of these people, something that helps you predict future behavior. I'm guessing the small crew of that jetliner didn't show up on your database."

"Ellen, are you telling me that you figured this out by yourself. I never once mentioned an algorithm."

"You didn't have to, Rick. I'm no secret agent man like you, but I can connect a few dots myself."

My head was spinning. I couldn't believe what Ellen just told me. I took out my cell phone.

"Buster, it's Rick. I'm with Ellen. We have to see you immediately."

"What's the big deal, Rick?" asked Ellen.

"I have to steal you away from your office for a while, hon. Come with me to meet Buster at Federal Plaza. What you just told me changes everything."

When we walked into Buster's office he was, no surprise, on the phone.

"Anything about the jet crew yet?" I asked.

Buster cleared his throat, looked at Ellen, then me.

"You've heard me say this a million times, Rick. Secrecy has nothing to do with trust. It's a question of a need to know. I trust your lovely wife here as much as I do you, but some things we shouldn't discuss."

"Well, you're about to hear something that's going to make you rethink a lot of things," I said. I nodded to Ellen.

"Buster," said Ellen, "I freaked out my hubby over lunch. Here's the story. I asked Rick if any of the crew members on the jet that hit the cruise ship were picked up by your algorithm. Rick looked at me with the same expression on his face that you're wearing now. No, Rick never mentioned it to me. I just pieced it together myself from what I thought were some obvious procedures."

"Ellen," said Buster, "we're talking about the most Top Secret matter possible. But since the cat's out of the bag, let's talk about the cat. How did you figure out that we use an algorithm?"

"Well I don't know all of the details, of course, but as I said, it seemed obvious to me that you guys have a huge database of persons of interest. And the only way to manage a large database is with a mathematical algorithm. I've designed dozens of them for my architectural work. It's *obvious*, Buster. And I'm guessing that your algorithm looks for all signs of jihadi indicators, such as visits to radical websites, mosque attendance, membership in organizations, and postings on the Internet."

"Buster," I said, "look at it this way. Ellen is just one person, a smart and observant person, but she's not a trained investigator. She just added up two plus two and sorted out what we're doing."

"So one bright non-spook has figured out our Top Secret process," said Buster.

"And if I figured it out, guys," said Ellen, "you can bet the jihadis have too."

CHAPTER SEVENTEEN

Thanksgiving Day came and went. Because of the hyper activity I'd been going through since 10/15, Ellen and I just had a quiet turkey dinner by ourselves. I try to think positive, but I wasn't sure what there was to be thankful for. Then I remembered – Ellen. When we said grace I thanked God for giving me Ellen. Thanksgiving wouldn't be the start of a long weekend because we had to be in Langley for a meeting at the CIA the next day.

＝＋＋＝

I hate meetings. One or two people can get a hell of a lot more done than sitting around a conference table with a bunch of talking heads. But this meeting was important, even necessary I had to admit. We were in Langley, Virginia, at CIA Headquarters. Director Carlini conducted the meeting. Ellen was there, along with Zeke, Buster, and me. A guy named Nigel Fleming was at the meeting representing Interpol, the International Criminal Police Organization.

It was the day after Thanksgiving, just over a week after the sinking of the cruise ship *The Sovereign of the Deep*. That attack was the subject of the meeting. Carlini asked Buster to give a rundown of what we knew. I hadn't seen Buster in a week, so I was as alert as everybody else to what he had to say.

"I can't believe it, but they found the black box," said Buster. "The searchers used a US Navy mini sub and located it under 300 feet of water. The Interpol folks gave it to us to interpret the results. Along with a couple of investigators from the National Transportation Safety Board, we now know what happened. As the jet climbed, it suddenly descended and aimed straight for the ship. Here's what we heard on the cockpit voice recorder:"

We listened to a couple of minutes of standard plane-to-tower chatter when suddenly a loud noise rang out. Buster put the replay on hold.

"What you just heard was a gunshot from a small caliber pistol. Our forensics people have confirmed it," said Buster. "Within five seconds, the plane began its sharp descent. From what you're about to hear, it's apparent that the captain shot the co-pilot."

"Allahu Akbar," shouted the pilot repeatedly.

"We've confirmed that the voice you just heard is that of Giuseppe Aldonzo, captain of the Airbus."

"Was Aldonzo on our radar, so to speak?" asked Director Carlini.

"No, he wasn't," said Buster, "but we've done a post-mortem on the man. If he was in our database, it may have given us a red flag, but only a small flag. It seems Captain Aldonzo converted to Islam five years ago when he was 38 years old. There was no public announcement about this. The Interpol investigators found out about his conversion only after interviewing people who knew him. So in retrospect, we did our analysis of all of Aldonzo's web activity and came up with zilch. No indication that he ever logged onto a radical website. The Interpol folks also checked out his religious activities. He must have worshipped from home because there is no record of his visiting a mosque. When they searched his apartment, they discovered all sorts of religious paraphernalia, but nothing that could be interpreted as radical. He was just a quiet Muslim. And here's what scares the shit out of me, if you'll pardon my Arabic. Given what we know about this guy, I don't think we could have gotten a search warrant from a FISA court, assuming for the sake of argument that he was an American. Our mighty algorithm wouldn't have blown a circuit over this man. He was just a Muslim, nothing more. But he also became a mass murderer."

"Buster," I said, "I think Ellen has something to say."

Everybody had already been briefed on Ellen's intuitive discovery of the algorithm.

"This pilot knew about your algorithm long before I figured it out," said Ellen. "He may not have thought of it as a computer algorithm, but he, and presumably his colleagues, knew that the CIA and FBI were getting good at predicting behavior, especially the behavior of latter-life converts to Islam. Look at it this way. A man converts to Islam at the age of 38. This wasn't a man who grew up in the religion. This was a guy who made a conscious decision in adulthood. Wouldn't you expect him to make it public? Wouldn't you expect to see the man visiting mosques? Wouldn't you expect this man to visit Islamic websites, radical or not? No, his conversion was discovered by police investigators after the fact. This was a guy who had a mission and realized the only way to accomplish it was to lurk in the shadows. Hey, guys, it's a simple process of reverse engineering. If we entitled your database, 'How to Catch a Jihadi,' all they need to do is come up with a simple two page pamphlet entitled, 'How Not to get Caught.' Hell, they wouldn't even need a friggin computer."

Buster slapped the table and put his face into his hands.

"I think all of us spooks are too close to our subject," said Buster. "Ellen has just uncovered something that could change the game. What I'm about to say I've discussed with Director Carlini, but now I'm making it known to you folks. Our algorithm has taken a vacation. Except for all the recent data that we plugged in after, I repeat *after*, the 10/15 attacks and the sinking of the cruise ship in New York, we've seen little output from the database. Just like Captain Giuseppe Aldonzo, jihadis, especially homegrown terrorists, are learning the art of hiding, or as Ellen put it, how to 'lurk in the shadows.' No matter how sophisticated our algorithm is, without a constant supply of data, it's just a computer program."

"Buster," said Carlini, "would you please give us a summary of your thoughts?"

"We're fucked."

CHAPTER EIGHTEEN

Phil Moretti, a structural engineer by trade, was enjoying a day fishing with his friend Bob McLaughlin in San Francisco Bay. McLaughlin was a professional photographer.

Moretti maneuvered the boat under the Golden Gate Bridge. McLaughlin, lying on a cot, clicked photos with his Nikon of the underside of the bridge. Moretti pointed out to him shots of special interest, especially the structure around the towers. With his powerful telephoto lens, he shot images that appeared to be only a few feet away.

Both men were touring the country and fishing. Fishing and photographing bridges. They had already fished the waters under all of the bridges in Manhattan, including the Brooklyn Bridge, the Verrazano, and the George Washington Bridge.

Their next fishing spot would be the Tacoma Narrows Bridge in Washington State. Then they would visit the Mackinac Bridge in Michigan, the Delaware Memorial Bridge, and the Walt Whitman Bridge in Philadelphia.

Moretti checked his watch and motored to a secluded cove off Tiburon. The afterdeck of the boat was covered by a canvas tarp or bimini, which prevented anyone ashore from seeing them on deck. As Moretti dropped the anchor, McLaughlin spread out two prayer rugs angled toward a compass heading that pointed to Mecca.

Moretti, age 36, and McLaughlin, age 28, had converted to Islam four years ago. Immediately after their conversion, they were approached by a man named Ali Bashara, who now went by the name Phillip Murphy.

Bashara/Murphy was a high-placed operative with al-Qaeda. Murphy counseled the men on radical Islam and his desire to see the dawn of a new caliphate on earth.

They didn't need much convincing, having already embraced political Islam and the rigors of jihad.

Murphy convinced them that they were not to make a public demonstration of their faith in any way, including the use of their new Muslim names. He counseled them to avoid any Islamic websites, not to wear traditional Muslim clothing, and not to worship at a mosque.

"Your faith shall live in the shadows," Murphy told them, "the glorious shadows of Allah."

>⊷⊶

Bob McLaughlin finished his fishing and photography trip with his friend Phil Moretti. He had photographed the major bridges in the United States, and looked forward to his next assignment where he could exercise his new skill, drone photography.

McLaughlin continued on his mission after saying goodbye to Moretti. His work would now focus on electrical substations across the country. According to his research there are 55,000 electric substations in the United States, but only nine are critical.

If one or more of those nine stations were put out of business on a hot summer day, it would be a dark day for America, he thought to himself, smiling.

He brought his 11-year-old nephew Andrew on his trip. What better way to avoid suspicion than to have child in tow? His brother and sister-in-law were delighted that Andrew would be getting photography lessons from a pro. McLaughlin had gotten to know and like Andrew and would often pick him up after church on Sunday to take him on photography trips.

His brother often asked him why he didn't drop in at church occasionally. He would just shrug and say that he liked to sleep late on Sundays. He never told his brother he had converted to Islam.

He picked up Andrew at his house in Yonkers, New York. Their first flight would be to San Jose, California, the site one of the nine critical substations. In April of 2013, he recalled, snipers fired on that substation, knocking out 17 giant transformers and essentially taking the facility out of service for a month.

A large park adjoined the fenced-in area. McLaughlin and Andrew sat on a park bench with their backs to the unit, located about 100 yards away. He piloted the drone helicopter skillfully over the station, flying it over a few other spots as well to avoid any possible suspicion. The helicopter was small, with a rotor span of only 12 inches. He flew it at a height of 200 feet, snapping pictures with the powerful lens of the attached camera.

He let Andrew try his hand at using the drone controls. It was just like playing a video game, his nephew thought. "These drones are a fabulous technology," he said to Andrew. "They make for wonderful picture-taking."

They are also excellent vehicles for delivering bombs, McLaughlin thought.

CHAPTER NINETEEN

"I don't know what you did to deserve a great woman like Ellen," said Buster, "but whatever it was, keep doing it. She showed us a hole in our defenses that you could pilot a ship through."

"Ellen's the best, and thanks for your compliment. I'll tell her – if you think she has a need to know, of course."

Buster laughed, for the first time in a long while.

We sat in my office at 26 Federal Plaza. Dr. Bennie Weinberg, our resident shrink, would join us shortly.

We heard a knock on the door and Bennie walked in. I noticed the bulge of a pistol on his chest. Although he's a NYPD psychiatrist, Bennie is also a detective. Since 10/15, no law enforcement official would even think about leaving his home without a gun.

We brought Bennie up to speed on Ellen's discovery of our compromised algorithm and the slowdown of data coming out of the jihadi database.

"As Buster so eloquently concluded our recent meeting at CIA headquarters," I said, " 'we're fucked.' Al-Qaeda is now two steps, maybe more like ten, in front of us. Unless we have data to feed the database, we may as well not have a database at all. The jihadis have figured out that they have to starve us for information, and they've also figured out how to do it. Without information, we have no way to predict anything, even with your brilliant psychiatric input."

"Did you two ever hear of positive thinking? We just have to go to Plan B."

"Okay, what's Plan B?" asked Buster.

"I haven't the foggiest idea, but that's what you spooks are for. I'm just a country shrink."

"Well, I do have a Plan B in mind," said Buster. "Old-fashioned spy work combined with old-fashioned police work. We have to get inside, more inside than we are already. There is no central registry of people who convert to Islam. It's not like you go to the county clerk's office and fill out a form. It's the same with any religion. If you convert from, say, Presbyterianism to Catholicism, your name isn't posted on a public database. The same with Islam. And, of course, some people convert to non-radical Islam. They just adopt a new religion."

"But if we have operatives inside," I said, "and I know Buster won't admit it if we do, how do we know they're trustworthy? How do we know they're not double agents?"

"We don't, except in a few cases, which I can't discuss," said Buster. "The idea isn't to have my people join mosques. I have a small army of 'journalists' as part of my team. They will interview people for articles about converts to Islam, and the articles will actually be published, with pseudonyms, of course. My thinking is that a conversion to Islam is an interesting news story. Nobody should suspect anything if a reporter just casually writes about religious conversions. The articles won't call them 'homegrown jihadis,' of course, just 'converts.' "

"There must be a lot of writing already out there on this subject, written by real journalists," said Bennie.

"Yes, there is, and our researchers scour the news every day looking for articles about people converting to Islam later in life. We also have people talking to leaders of other religions, asking questions such as 'has anybody in your church ever converted to Islam?' We get a lot of interesting answers."

"So, Buster," I said, "if I hear you correctly, we're not completely cut off from homegrown jihadi information, just that it's gotten tougher to find."

"That's exactly what I'm saying, Rick. It's like fossil hunting. The fossils are there – we just have to uncover them."

"Don't forget to research the psychological journals," said Bennie. "There's been a lot of politically incorrect discussions in the mental health community about converts to Islam. Some people question whether a later-in-life conversion could mask an underlying psychological problem. It drives the lefties nuts, but I think it's a legitimate area of inquiry. I was going to write a paper on it myself, but I figured it best not to compromise my reputation or identity. Also, I mentioned it to the NYPD Police Commissioner, and he advised me that he'd place my nuts in a vise if I wrote the article."

Buster scribbled notes.

"Bennie, you're a fucking genius. But you already know that."

CHAPTER TWENTY

My husband still isn't convinced that MacPherson International didn't have something to do with all of the attacks, and neither am I, even after the investigation. I feel uncomfortable spying on a client, especially a big client who pays big fees, but everything that's happened since 10/15 has put me squarely on the side of protecting our country. Maybe I'm turning into a secret agent type like Rick. He finally convinced me to carry a pistol – and yes, I got a concealed carry permit. Rick even gave me intensive training on the use of an assault rifle, an AK-47. I don't like to carry a gun, but suddenly I'm on the inside of all this stuff. It might sound crazy, but I have a feeling I may need my gun to protect Rick someday. I would have no problem shooting any bastard who lifted a finger against my Rick.

I sat in the waiting room adjacent to Angus MacPherson's office. I decided to chat with Magda, his Middle Eastern assistant.

"So, Magda, what do you think of the plans for the big shopping center project?"

She looked at me as if I just tried to steal her purse.

"Why do you ask me this?" said Magda.

"Oh, just wondering. It's such an exciting project I figured you'd have some thoughts about it."

"I have no such thoughts," said Magda, observing me through squinted eyes. "I come here and I do my job."

"I think it's a great idea to have one big security firm in charge of all the sites. That should save a lot of money. What do you think?" I'd be damned if I was going to let Magda off the hook.

She gave me another look, a look that made me glad I was wearing a pistol. Then she asked me a question.

"Why are you so concerned about our security force? Aren't you an architect? Do architects always ask so many questions?"

A buzzer on her desk sounded and Magda picked up the phone.

"Mr. MacPherson will see you now, Mrs. Bellamy," said Magda, looking at me as if I were a rattlesnake that just dropped in for a visit.

⭒╌ ╌⭒

"So good to see you again, lassie. Please help yourself to some coffee."

He asked about the schedule for the shopping centers.

"We're good to go, Mr. MacPherson, I mean Angus. From my view, I don't see a problem with opening all of the centers on the day we planned. At the risk of annoying you, I still think we should give up the idea of the sloping stainless steel ceilings. You're giving up so much valuable retail space."

"Yes, I know, lass, but let's go forward as planned. And no, I'm not annoyed with you. I know you're thinking of my best interests."

He shrugged his shoulders and showed that same sad look as he did at our last meeting, like he was resigned to something. I knew damned well that he agreed with me. He's one of the most successful businessmen in the country if not the world, and we were going forward with cutesy artistic plans that were just plain stupid – and he wasn't telling me why. Maybe I was reading too much into this, but I wished to God I could figure out why he was committed to a bad design.

I finished my update, gathered my drawings, and headed for the door after a warm handshake from Angus.

Magda, my waiting room buddy, gave me a parting look of friendliness, like a scorpion observing a beetle. I patted my hip and felt comforted that my Glock was there.

CHAPTER TWENTY ONE

"Hey, Rick. Long time no see."

Frank Palmara, my old friend from the FBI Academy, popped into my office with his usual burst of enthusiasm. I don't know why, but Frank always seems excited about something. It probably helps his career. He's a good guy, and I was sorry we didn't work together any more. He was assigned to headquarters in D.C.

"So what have you been up to, Frank? It's been a year since I last saw you."

"Just a lot of boring gumshoe work. Nothing glamorous and exciting like counterterrorism. I envy you, Rick."

"Really? Maybe you'd like to join me in a bowl of Maalox. This glamorous shit makes me afraid to turn on the TV in the morning."

"Well, what you do is a lot more exciting than working and re-working stuff like the MacPherson case."

What the hell did he just say? My professional gut told me that Frank just blurted out something he wasn't supposed to. My mind was suddenly on high alert, but I had to act casual so Frank wouldn't realize he just blew something.

"Oh, yeah, the MacPherson case," I said, as if I knew what he was talking about. "What's new with that?"

"Nothing, as usual. His wife and daughter were kidnapped by a group we think is affiliated with al-Qaeda. We're stuck. He seems totally distraught over it, but he doesn't want us to do anything clandestine to try to locate them. He gets photos and videos regularly, showing that they're okay, but he seems like he's walking on eggshells. And the worst part is he won't tell us about their demands."

Holy shit. It's hard to act casual when a bomb blows up in your face, and one had just blown up in mine.

"Frank, you mean that one of the most powerful men in the country is a kidnap victim, a man subject to coercion, which is what kidnapping is all about, and this is a fucking secret?"

"This comes right from the director's office. No publicity. Completely hush, hush. Shit, I probably shouldn't be telling *you* about this," Frank observed accurately.

"Don't worry, Frank. Your secret is good with me," I lied.

I didn't tell him anything about my part in the investigation of MacPherson International. Time to play this close to the vest. I needed to talk to Ellen.

⟞⟊ ⟊⟝

"Can we have lunch, hon? There's something I've got to talk to you about."

"Is everything okay, Rick? You sound troubled."

"I am. I've got to see you. How about I order sandwiches and we'll meet in my office. We need privacy, and you'll find out why when I see you."

Ellen walked into my office at 12:15. She wore Chanel N°5, my favorite perfume, which always distracts me. But I had to focus.

"I can't believe this, but MacPherson's wife and daughter were kidnapped by al-Qaeda. It happened about eight months ago. For some reason, it's completely Top Secret. It's never been leaked to the press. You met with MacPherson this morning, didn't you?"

"Yes. Oh my God, Rick, this explains a lot. I'm not sure what it explains, but let me tell you about my meeting with him. I told you that I think he agrees with me that the shopping mall plans are nuts. He's giving up over $3.5 million a year in rent because of the weird ceilings. I politely reminded him about my opinion again this morning, and I got the same reaction. He looked resigned, almost sad."

"Like he's not the guy calling the shots?"

"Yes, you're right, that's exactly how he acted. Now that you tell me his wife and daughter are being held for ransom, I'm positive he's *not* calling the shots. He's a man in a vise, and al-Qaeda's squeezing it. But I still don't understand why anybody, al-Qaeda included, would want to give up so much rental space just for a visionary design."

"Anything else about the meeting that you found interesting? Anything out of the ordinary?"

"Yeah, his assistant, Magda. The last time I met with MacPherson, I casually asked where Magda was from because of her heavy accent. He just mumbled something about her being from the Middle East. So today, while waiting for MacPherson, I decided to have a chat with the mysterious Magda. I could have had a more interesting conversation with the wall. I asked her about her thoughts on the plans, and also about the in-house security. She treated me like I was a burglar. She wouldn't answer a question or give her opinion on anything. Nothing I can put my finger on, but that woman gives me the creeps."

"Somebody is calling the shots for MacPherson International," I said, "and I don't think it's MacPherson. But I'm totally stumped about the ceilings. Why the hell would he lose so much rental space because of a design? Put on your architect's hat, Ellen. Do those sloped steel ceilings serve any purpose at all?"

"No purpose that I can figure out, Rick, other than aesthetics. But I'll keep thinking. I gotta get back to the office."

And I've got to get inside this MacPherson case, I thought. Every time I learn something new about MacPherson, I hear a bomb ticking. But what is it?

⊶ ⊷

"Hey, Frank, it's Rick. Glad you're still here. Could you drop by my office? I need to talk to you about something important."

Frank Palmara walked into my office, but without his usual enthusiasm.

"Frank, let me get to the point. I've got to get inside the MacPherson matter. My wife is the architect in charge of his planned shopping centers, and something isn't right. I can't go into detail now, but my team needs to get inside the case. And, because the last thing I want to do is fuck up your career, I want *you* to suggest it to Director Watson. You don't have to tell her that you told me about the MacPherson kidnapping. Tell her that I started talking about my wife's work and that I seemed suspicious."

"What if I refuse, Rick?"

"Then, my friend, and you are my friend, I will go to Watson myself. I'll just tell her I heard it from somebody. Frank, this is about counterterrorism. This is about national security. Please make this happen."

"I'll do it right now, Rick. And thanks for covering my ass."

⊶ ⊷

Frank Palmara, bless him, worked fast. At 3 p.m. I got word from Sarah Watson's assistant that she wanted to see me. Watson was visiting the New York headquarters.

"Hello, Rick. Please have a seat. Your old friend Frank Palmara suggests that I bring you in on a case. It's a Top Secret matter. About eight months ago, Angus MacPherson's wife and daughter were kidnapped by al-Qaeda. I ordered no leaks to anyone because the situation is so sensitive. I know that your wife, Ellen, is the architect for a big MacPherson project. Frank thinks you're on to something. Tell me about it."

I faked surprise at what she told me, concerned about the career of my friend Frank Palmara.

I discussed the bizarre design for the buildings and the enormous sacrifice of retail space for no good reason. I also told her Ellen suspected that MacPherson was being coerced by someone and that my hunch was al-Qaeda.

"What should we do, Rick? Give me your suggestions."

"I recommend that we bring in Buster, that CIA guy you met, and also Bennie Weinberg. I want Bennie to interview MacPherson, as a NYPD detective or FBI agent, not as a psychiatrist. MacPherson won't be surprised that another detective wants to interview him. I want Bennie's opinion of MacPherson's truthfulness. It could lead us in an interesting direction."

"I'll call Bennie and explain it to him. Obviously he should be briefed, by you and Ellen. Then I'll personally call MacPherson and give Bennie some cover."

"Thanks, Director Watson. I'll keep you in the loop on everything, of course."

"Rick, good work. Keep it up. Let me know about Bennie's meeting with MacPherson. I'm beginning to think you're onto something."

⇒⊹⇐

"Bennie, if we ever needed a bullshit detector, it's now," I said.

Ellen and I met with Bennie in my office.

"Something's missing, Bennie," said Ellen. "We've told you about the weird design for Angus MacPherson's big shopping center project. From a business point of view, the plan is absurd. As an architect, part of my job is to make sure the client is served well, and I've told MacPherson more times than I can remember that this plan is a loser, a money loser. With only one floor of retail space in each of the five planned buildings, I've calculated that MacPherson International will lose $3.6 million a year on rentals, all because he wants to have this strange one-story design with inwardly sloping steel ceilings. The buildings will look beautiful, but at an enormous cost."

"What did MacPherson say when you tried to talk him out of the plans?" asked Bennie.

"That's the strange part of this whole story. As I told Rick, MacPherson seems to agree with me, but he acts, I don't know, like he's powerless to do anything about it. He looks resigned, almost sad. It's as if he's going through the motions with something he doesn't want. Rick thinks MacPherson may not be calling his own shots."

"Ellen, Rick told me this morning that MacPherson's wife and daughter were kidnapped eight months ago. Without even talking to the man, I can tell you that he's definitely not in charge of his own mind. From what I've heard, the MacPhersons had a long and loving relationship. The whole idea behind any kidnapping is coercion. The kidnappers either have the typical demand, like a ransom, or they want to somehow control the behavior and decision-making of the victim."

"Keep in mind, Bennie," I said, "that MacPherson is absolutely against any kind of publicity. The kidnapping itself was Top Secret information here at the FBI. The CIA knew nothing about it. I just found out about it the other day by accident. Director Watson told MacPherson that you're one of the agents who knows about the kidnapping. If you just brought it up, we're worried that he'd freak out. I'm guessing that al-Qaeda has a tight leash on this guy."

"Has anybody come up with a theory that this MacPherson business may have anything to do with the recent terrorist attacks?" Bennie said.

"We don't know," I said. "None of us can figure out what these shopping mall projects can have to do with terrorism. Maybe al-Qaeda is just looking for an investment."

"A stupid investment," said Ellen. "Even a camel driver can see that these malls are designed wrong."

"First things first," I said. "Bennie, we need you to determine if MacPherson's lying. We have to find out what he knows, or at least what he's thinking. But I'll settle for an up or down vote from you. Is he bullshitting or not?"

⊫⊣ ⊢⊨

I may be a smart psychiatrist, but this case has me stumped. I'm about to meet with a wealthy and powerful guy whose emotions are on the ropes. He wants to protect his family, but it looks like somebody else is making decisions. We're guessing it's al-Qaeda. But why? Nobody has an answer for that question.

Okay, my job as "Bennie the Bullshit Detector" – I'm starting to hate that nickname – is to put the guy at ease and get him talking. I plan to do that by telling him it's just a routine follow-up call. I won't tell him that I'm a psychiatrist, only that I'm a detective on loan to the FBI. That part is true, of course. It just doesn't make sense to let him know I'm a shrink.

"Mr. MacPherson will see you now," said the woman whose nameplate on her desk announced her as Magda. She was as cuddly as a hornet, just as Ellen described her. It was clear that seeing an FBI agent like me wasn't the high point of her day.

"Good morning, Mr. Weinberg," said MacPherson with a heavy Scottish brogue as he held out his hand. "It seems part of every week includes a visit from the FBI."

"Director Watson has told you, sir, that I'm one of the few agents who's aware of the status of your wife and daughter."

"Yes, she has, laddie."

I had to smile. Nobody's ever called me "laddie" before.

"Mr. MacPherson, as we told you, my visit today is just a routine follow up to our continuing investigation. I'm sure you've noticed that detectives, including FBI agents, tend to ask a lot of questions. And we also have a habit of repeating a lot of questions. So please pardon me if I seem to be treading over old ground."

"Not at all, lad. I've spoken to so many of you that I'm thinking of recording my answers so you don't have to ask them again."

Ellen was right. This guy was charming, with a self-effacing sense of humor.

"So if I may, Mr. MacPherson, I'd like to talk about the design for your new shopping mall projects. To the casual observer, and of course there's no such thing as a casual observer who's an FBI agent, the design of these malls doesn't appear to make much sense from a business point of view. Hey, I'm no architect, but as an investigator I always wonder about things that seem to be out of the ordinary, things that don't fit. Do you care to comment, sir?"

"Well, lad, I've been around for more years than I'd like to admit. I've made a lot of money and my real estate developments always turn out successful. But this time I've opted for beauty over practical business. Maybe you can call it an old man's legacy, but for once in my life, I've turned my eyes toward art."

I noticed that he began to perspire. When he said that bit about opting for beauty, he didn't look me in the eye. As he blabbered on about how pretty the buildings would look, he stared at his lap. He also rubbed the side of his nose, repeatedly, and cleared his throat so many times I thought a moth had flown in. If I could choose a video for a lecture on lie detecting, this would be perfect. Angus MacPherson was bullshitting me.

It was so obvious that MacPherson was lying, I could have ended the interview there. Rick Bellamy said my main job was to determine if our Scottish friend was telling the truth. Well, he was lying, but I wasn't about to let an opportunity go. I wanted to see *why* he was lying.

"Mr. MacPherson, you don't have to convince me that leaving behind a legacy is important to a man such as yourself. You're one of the best-known and revered businessmen in the country, and you're turning yourself toward something lasting. I get it, sir. Hell, look at what Andrew Carnegie did with the New York Public Library system. He made his millions but decided it was time to make a statement for posterity. But if you could just clarify something for me, and I'm sorry to be going beyond my bounds here, but I'm just trying to make sense of this in my own head. Why not commission a famous sculptor and donate beautiful statues to parks throughout the country? Or why not hire a bunch of talented artists and rehabilitate some old dilapidated real estate? Pardon me, Mr. MacPherson, but it seems that you could do so much more with your money than sink it into an economically crippled shopping mall project."

His demeanor changed. He looked me square in the eyes. I had a feeling he was trying to connect with me but didn't quite know how. He picked up a set of drawings off the desk, stood up, and walked over next to me. He opened the folder, and there in front of me was a message, printed in a large font.

"This room is bugged. Meet me at my house in Scarsdale tomorrow at 2 p.m. Take a rental car, not an official vehicle. Enter under the *porte cachere* around back. Wear a disguise and bring agent Bellamy and his wife Ellen with you. They should also wear disguises."

Holy shit! I had no idea that he knew Ellen and Rick were married. MacPherson then went on to talk about how beautiful the plans looked. He was obviously putting on an act for whoever was monitoring the bugs in the room.

"Well, they certainly are beautiful plans, sir. I don't know why I'm so concerned about the design," I lied to the bugs. "I won't tie up any more of your day, and I thank you for taking the time to see me."

I slipped MacPherson's note into my pocket. As I left the office, I smiled at Magda. She looked at me as if I were a cockroach.

⊷⊷

Bennie walked into my office at noon. Ellen was already there with me. To save time, I ordered lunch for our meeting.

"So, Bennie," I said, "is Angus MacPherson hiding something from us?"

"Yes, pure bullshit, but it gets better. He wants to see us, the three of us, at his house in Scarsdale tomorrow afternoon at 2 p.m. He specifically asked me to bring Agent Bellamy—and get this— agent Bellamy's wife, Ellen. He knows you two are married. He knows that his architect is married to an FBI agent. What's more, his office is bugged, and that's why he wants to meet us at his house. Here's a note he showed me. He wants us to wear disguises and gave specific instructions about where to enter. He doesn't want us to use an official car. Tomorrow afternoon we're going to learn something. Something that may turn this case upside down."

"How do we know his house isn't bugged?" asked Ellen.

"Whatever Angus Macpherson is, he's not stupid. I'm sure the place is clean. He wants to open up to us."

CHAPTER TWENTY TWO

Joseph Portman, aka Abbas Muktada met with his mentor Phillip Murphy, aka Ali Bashara.

"Congratulations Joseph. When you greeted me you didn't call me brother Ali. You are catching on to the new rules. Today I have something important to discuss with you, the most important mission you will ever have been involved in."

"Can you give me any details, Phil?"

"Not now. As you know, the Committee discloses things only when they must, not sooner. But I can tell you this: you will be instrumental in the largest undertaking since 10/15."

"Can you tell me when it will happen?"

"An event will occur the day after the infidel Thanksgiving next year, and you will be a key to making it happen."

CHAPTER TWENTY THREE

I drove our rental car up the long driveway to Angus MacPherson's house in Scarsdale, New York. It was a Victorian mansion perched atop a hill on a five-acre plot. As MacPherson's note requested, I drove around to the back of the mansion and pulled under a *porte cachere*. A butler opened the doors and escorted us into the enormous entry hallway. The walls were hung with original art works and antiques lined the floor. The place gushed wealth.

The butler asked us to follow him into a large den, more like a drawing room. He directed us to chairs around a large table, which looked to me to be mahogany, but it was probably something more exotic.

After a couple of minutes, Angus MacPherson entered the room. He walked up to each of us and, with a forced smile, shook our hands.

"So, lassie, ye found yourself a secret agent man," he said to Ellen with a pleasant smile.

"I never keep it quiet, Angus. It just never came up in conversation between you and me."

"Pay it no mind, lass. I'm actually delighted that my charming architect married a man with a skeptical eye. So to paraphrase a classic line from an old movie, I suppose you're all wondering why I've gathered you here today."

"Mr. MacPherson, I think you just summed up our thinking," I said.

"Well then, let's be perfectly open with each other. You're all aware of the kidnapping of my wife, Margo, and my daughter, Jane. Margo and I have been married for 51 years, and to be perfectly honest with you, I'm devastated. After Jane graduated from Princeton, she went to Harvard Business School where she got an MBA. I miss her as much as I miss Margo. She'll eventually take over MacPherson International. Please ask me any questions about this part of the MacPherson story."

"Mr. MacPherson," said Bennie, "the whole idea behind a kidnapping is usually a ransom, either in money or in action. What have they demanded from you?"

"Good question, Dr. Ben. Oh yes, I know you're a psychiatrist. They haven't placed a demand for money on the table. But they have inserted themselves into my shopping mall project."

"Excuse me," I said, "but when you say 'they,' are you referring to al-Qaeda or ISIS or some other terrorist organization?"

"That, lad, opens up a strange tale, indeed. Shortly after the kidnapping, I was approached by a pleasant young man, maybe 35 years old or so. I fully expected some bearded bastard with a sword clenched in his teeth. His name is Ahmed Farooq, but he looked like a typical American fella. He even had blond hair. He approached me as a businessman. You folks aren't the only ones who know how to spy, so I had my people check out Mr. Farooq. It seems he's from Chicago, and his real name is Walter Benning. He graduated from Northwestern University where he majored in economics. I expected him to give me a number, a ransom demand. Instead, he engaged me in a lengthy conversation about my shopping mall projects. He even had drawings."

"Did those drawings show the one-story design with the sloping steel ceilings?" asked Ellen.

"Yes, lass, the design you hate. It's also the design that I hate. I can't remember how many times you tried to talk me out of it. It isn't a design meant for business. It's a design meant for, well, I have no idea what it's meant for. As you've pointed out many times, Ellen, it's sheer stupidity from any rational business point of view. But there isn't a hell of a lot I can do about it, is there? The charming Mr. Farooq has made it quite clear that the design of the shopping malls is their ransom. Either I capitulate and agree to the plans, or Margo and Jane will be killed. Farooq actually used the word 'beheaded,' the cold-blooded swine. So, Ellen, I hope that explains why I'm pressing forward with a stupid plan. I either follow the plan or I lose Margo and Jane."

"Angus, here's the question, the really big question," said Ellen. "Do you have any idea what this design is all about? There has to be something more to it than a desire to lose rental income. It's important enough for them to kidnap the family of a powerful man. What are they up to?"

"Ellen, I've agonized over that question for eight long months. I have absolutely no idea."

"When will the deal be done?" asked Bennie. "Did Farooq give you a date when Margo and Jane will be returned?"

"Yes, the Monday after Thanksgiving and three days after Black Friday, the biggest shopping day of the year. Part of the deal is that I open all of the malls no later than Black Friday."

"Is part of the deal that you advertise the openings for Black Friday?" I asked.

"Yes, Rick. Not only am I required to advertise the openings, something that the retailers themselves would normally be responsible for, but they also want me to give a cash-back bonus to each tenant to help pack the shoppers in. The average number of shoppers at peak capacity should be about 15,000 per mall, or 75,000 people at any given time in all of the malls.

⯀

"Wait, hold everything," I said. "This plan isn't only stupid or bad business. It's completely insane. Farooq must know that he can't enter into a legally enforceable contract with you. The law says you can't enter a binding contract under coercion. Your family being held hostage is obviously coercion. All of the properties are in your name, or MacPherson International and a few banks. It's obvious that they can't take you to court. Could it be that al-Qaeda's plan is to see you stand up to your part of the deal, only to get the thrill of watching you lose money? Simple question – what's in it for them?"

"Rick, I simply do not know."

"Angus," Ellen said, "can you tell us anything about MacPherson Security Corporation?"

"I was about to bring that up. I began the operation about five years ago. It seemed like a good idea to have our own security at all of our buildings. I soon realized it was a bad idea. We made a profit from renting our security forces to other businesses, but using them in-house was becoming a complicated mess. I was about to put the firm up for sale when Margo and Jane were kidnapped. Mr. Farooq put a stop to my plans to sell the business. It seems that having an in-house security operation is very attractive to Farooq and his colleagues."

"Are you still hiring?" I asked. "My guess is that you'll need a lot more people to patrol the five shopping malls next year."

"Good question, lad. The answer is I have no idea. I have nothing at all to do with our security business. All hiring and firing is controlled by managers who were hired – not by me – in the past eight months."

He could see the shocked expressions on our faces.

"A related question, Angus," said Ellen. "Did you personally hire Magda, your assistant?"

"No, she's one of them. Her job, apparently, is to keep an eye on me. Did you ever think I would hire such a vile creature?"

"Next year something is going to happen," said Ellen, "something big. Black Friday is going to take on a new meaning."

"But what?" I said.

Nobody came up with an answer.

CHAPTER TWENTY FOUR

Zeke, Bennie, and I met with Buster in his office three days after the MacPherson meeting. Bennie and I brought Buster and Zeke up to speed on what we learned. I had hoped that Ellen could be at our meeting, but she was out of town that morning.

"So we're stuck with a total mystery," I said. "MacPherson's strings are pulled by al-Qaeda, at least we think it's al-Qaeda. He doesn't know any more about the strange building designs than we do. All we know is it's a puzzle that doesn't fit together. If we can figure out what al-Qaeda can get out of this, we'll know what to do, if not how to do it, whatever 'it' is."

There was a loud knock on the door. Buster unlocked and opened it, and Ellen walked right past him. She sat down at the conference table and took a deep breath. She seemed to be bursting with something to tell us.

"It's a blast concentrator," said Ellen.

The four of us just stared at her.

"What are you talking about, hon?" I said.

"I just got back from West Point. I met with Jeanine Smith, a college friend of mine who's an engineering professor at the academy. Jeanine's an expert in designing military structures, and it just popped into my mind that she may have a clue about the design of the shopping mall plans. It turns out she had more than a clue. I didn't discuss any names of course, but I showed her the plans and asked her if she could see any possible use for them. After looking at the plans for about a minute, she freaked out. She referred to the stainless steel sloping ceilings as 'blast concentrators.' "

"What is a blast concentrator?" asked Buster. "It sounds familiar, but please explain."

"One large bomb set off in the middle of any of the shopping centers will kill everyone there. The initial shock wave from the bomb will be reflected back by the sloped steel ceilings, pulverizing, and I do mean pulverizing, all life in the building. According to Jeanine, the only good news for anyone present is that they'll die instantly. And remember, Angus said he expects 75,000 shoppers across all five buildings at any given time. 75,000 people who will be killed in an instant."

None of us said anything for over a minute, our minds contemplating what Ellen had just told us.

"And remember, all security will be in-house," I said. "Whoever controls security also controls anything that comes into the buildings."

⤜⟞ ⟝⤏

"So let's get this straight," I said. "Al-Qaeda, using MacPherson's fortune and real estate assets, wants to pull off a terror spectacular the day after Thanksgiving next year by killing 75,000 people. Let's connect a few dots.

On October 15, they hit at commuter transportation. Dot one – how people get to work.

That same day, they attacked office buildings, places where millions of Americans go every day. Dot two – what happens when people get to their jobs.

Then they sunk the *Ocean Mariner* and *The Sovereign of the Deep*. Dot three – hit the vacation and leisure industry.

Between now and next Black Friday there may be more dots, but even if not, the Black Friday event will be a huge dot – American retail trade, a gigantic part of our economy."

"Anybody beginning to see a pattern?" said Buster. "Commuter transportation, office space, travel and leisure, and if our thinking is correct, retail trade. These scumbags are systematically picking apart our economy and culture."

"Folks, if I may suggest," said Bennie. "Let's look at some dots that aren't on the map yet, some institutions or areas of commerce they haven't hit yet."

"Infrastructure," said Ellen. "They could target the electrical grid. And what about bridges?"

"Agriculture," said Buster. "They could go after large farms, or the trucks and trains that haul the produce."

"Let's keep in mind," said Bennie, "that the events since 10/15 have been technically simple. Suicide bomb vests, a large bomb on a pilot boat, a jet loaded with fuel. None of these attacks were nearly as sophisticated as 9/11. If we're right about the MacPherson shopping malls, that operation will be the only event that's complicated."

"But there are a lot of simple acts of terror that they can inflict," I said. "How complicated is it to release a bag of anthrax from a small airplane? How about pouring a sack of poison into a reservoir? And, as Ellen pointed out, how difficult would it be to hit a bunch of main power supply substations? They need two things to pull any of these plans off. First, they need a person willing to commit suicide – and they seem to have an endless supply of those people. Second, they use 'homegrown' terrorists, people who won't arouse suspicion. We've learned recently that there are plenty of locally grown jihadis around, and not just here in the States. Because they've learned the trick of keeping the local creeps under the radar, Buster's algorithm is of limited use. There's one thing worse than not knowing something. It's not knowing that you don't know."

"Buster," said Bennie, "you're the resident spook here. Is there a way to get inside?"

"Well, we *are* inside," said Buster. "I can't go into more detail than that, but we have operatives under cover. Since the database has been choked off, the only data we're feeding it comes from our inside people."

⟩⟨ ⟩⟨

"If I could make a suggestion," said Deputy FBI Agent Ellen, "I think we should focus on what we intend to do about the MacPherson shopping mall plot."

Ellen, God bless her, was taking her provisional agent role quite seriously. A good thing, I thought, because she's probably smarter than all of us.

"That will be incredibly tricky," said Buster. "MacPherson told us he's basically cut off from the operations of his security company. We've got to find out how they intend to get the bombs in and when they intend to do it. The only possible way I see it is from the inside. I'm not divulging any CIA secrets here, I'm just speculating. I don't want the outcome to be a gunfight, not in crowded shopping centers. We've got to find out who controls the bombs and how many bombs will be in each location. And to add to those complications, try this thought on for size. We have no idea what else the enemy has in store between now and the MacPherson plot."

"What we've learned in the last few weeks," said Bennie, "is that we're blind and deaf. We can't afford to be dumb."

"I have a gut feeling that al-Qaeda's plans are at an advanced stage," said Zeke.

CHAPTER TWENTY FIVE

"Peace be upon you, brother Bashara."

"I remind you, Joseph, you are to use my American name, Phillip Murphy. And I also remind you that you must no longer call yourself Abbas Muktada. You are Joseph Portman. And when you meet a brother, do not say 'peace be upon you.' The last time I saw you, the new rules seemed to have sunk in, but now you're back to your lax ways. Am I clear?"

"Yes, broth...I mean Phillip. This will take some getting used to."

"And get used to it we must. It is now my pleasure to tell you about your new job. I saw in your file that you've had some police training, and it will now become useful to you, and to us. Next Monday, you will report to the office of MacPherson Security Corporation in New York. You are to report to a Bob Margano, a brother who used to go by the name Ali Bukdama before we changed the rules.

"You will soon be assigned to a major project. I cannot tell you the details of the project now, but you will learn about it over the next few months. All I can tell you is that you will be a key player in a glorious event that will happen next year."

"Is this company connected to MacPherson International, the big real estate developer?"

"Yes, Joe. Are you familiar with the company?"

"I've read about it in newspapers and magazines. The infidel in charge is a man named Angus MacPherson. From what I've read, he's one of the smartest businessmen in the country. Won't such a powerful man get in the way of whatever our plans may be?"

"Don't worry yourself about Angus MacPherson, Joe. Let's just say we have a special relationship with him. Oh, and by the way, don't use the word 'infidel.' Remember, our mission is to bring glory to Allah in the shadows."

"Perhaps, Phil, we shouldn't say things like 'bring glory to Allah.'"

"You are absolutely correct. Thank you for bringing that to my attention."

"I will see you next week after you meet with Bob Margano and begin your new job. It will be the most important mission of your life."

CHAPTER TWENTY SIX

I got home at 7:30 p.m. Ellen greeted me at the door wearing only one of my white dress shirts. I don't know what it is about a man's dress shirt on a beautiful woman, but it makes me nuts. She put her arms around my neck and blew a kiss into my ear. We stood in the entrance hallway of our apartment and made out like a couple of kids. As I held her closer to me, I sensed that she could feel that I was in the mood too. Reluctantly, I pulled back slightly.

"Hey, let me shower away the stress of the day. Why don't you pop a cork and pour us some wine."

"That's not the only thing I'm going to pop."

I wonder if all architects have such a way with words.

I climbed into the shower, letting the water and soap rinse away the day's stress. I thought about nothing but the evening to come. After a longer than usual shower, I climbed out and toweled off, opening the door slightly to release the steam.

"Hey, hon. I want you to take that shirt off because I'm going to wear it tomorrow. But please come here and take it off in front of me so I can make sure you don't wrinkle it. Hon? Ellen? Hey, where are you?"

She must be playing one of her sexy hiding games, I thought.

I went to the master suite. Maybe she was in the bathroom. Not there. I walked all over our 2,400 square foot apartment. Still no sign of her.

I glanced at the doorway, the last place I thought to look. Oh Dear God, the door was ajar!

I opened the door fully and looked down the hallway. I ran back inside to get my gun and badge. I'm in excellent physical condition, but my heart pounded like I was an old man who just ran a marathon. I sprinted to the elevator, wearing only my terrycloth robe. Marty, the doorman, must have seen something. Marty sees everything.

When the door opened on the first floor, I got out, turned right, and started to run to the lobby. Three cops stood there, guns drawn. I kept mine in the pocket of my robe. Like all law enforcement people, I'd been trained not to cause an incident in a confusing situation.

"Hey, buddy, freeze," said one of the cops, pointing a gun at me.

"It's okay, Mickey," said another one of the cops. "I know this guy. He's FBI and he lives here.

Hey Rick, do you know anything about this?"

I saw he was standing over Marty's body. His head was half blown away by a gunshot wound.

"My wife's been kidnapped," I barely managed to croak out. "Less than five minutes ago."

"Holy shit. What was she wearing?" he asked as he pressed on his radio. I told him she wore a men's white shirt and nothing else.

"That should help narrow it down."

"Woman missing and presumed kidnapped from 2 Fifth Avenue less than five minutes ago," he yelled to the desk officer who picked up the call.

"Yeah? Wow, okay. Keep me posted, Jack. Her husband, Rick Bellamy, the FBI guy, is with me. You know Rick."

I looked at him with eyes like saucers and put out my hands, signaling, "So what happened?"

"Somebody called in an alarm a few minutes ago reporting a woman matching your wife's description and manner of dress. A man was seen shoving her into the back of a dark colored sedan. I hate to say this, Rick, but half the fucking sedans in this city are dark colored. The caller didn't have the presence of mind to note the license plate. Jack Flynn back at the precinct is putting out an APB to be on the lookout for a dark colored sedan with a blonde in the back. We don't have a lot to go on, buddy. I'm sorry. What can I do for you?"

"Let's get my apartment dusted for prints. Just basic shit, I know. The bastard probably wore gloves."

This wasn't the evening I planned.

⇒⋅⇐

I called Buster on his cell phone.

"Open the door, Rick. I'm standing here right outside your apartment."

"How did you know?"

"I just picked it up on the police radio. They gave her name."

"Rick, I know what you're going through. I need you to think. Try to think. I want all your thoughts so we can start to piece this together."

"Buster, this has got to be connected with MacPherson's wife and daughter. I'm taking a wild guess here, but I think they want Ellen to talk to the MacPherson women. I don't think this is a typical kidnapping, and I doubt they're holding Ellen for ransom. They want to use the MacPherson women to get Ellen to talk about the shopping center plan. They want to know what we know about

114

the plan for Black Friday. Who better to find that out from than the architect herself? They're figuring that Ellen will want to assure the MacPhersons that the good guys are working on the case. If I'm right, Ellen will be brought to wherever the MacPherson women are being held captive. But what the hell does that theory get us? We have no idea where they are. Somewhere in the Middle East probably, but who the fuck knows?"

"Rick, we know where the MacPhersons are."

"What? Where?"

"Tenafly, New Jersey."

"Why didn't you tell me this?"

"I just found out this afternoon. One of our operatives spotted them. They're at an al-Qaeda safe house. I should say it's a place that al-Qaeda *thinks* is a safe house."

Buster's phone sounded. He answered the call, but all he said was, "Holy shit, got it, got it. Keep me posted."

Buster grabbed me by the shoulders and looked me in the eyes.

"That was my guy watching the safe house. Your theory's correct, Rick. A car just brought Ellen there."

The simple knowledge that we knew where she was washed over me like warm water.

"Now what?" I asked.

"Rick, we're in. We're in deep. One of my operatives arrived at the house today. This guy has been under deep cover for over a year. We're inside, Rick. I don't know if that makes you feel any better, but it's a start."

"Any thoughts on a rescue?"

"Of course, but it won't be easy. The place is heavily guarded, as you can imagine. I've been involved in more kidnapping situations than I can remember, but this won't be a typical hostage negotiation. Once they know we're on to them, all hell will break loose. We want to be the ones who inflict the hell."

CHAPTER TWENTY SEVEN

I cannot believe what's happening to me. I'm still wearing only a man's shirt. One of the turds shoved me into a room and threw me a pair of slacks, a sweater, a pair of loafers, and a burqa. He ordered me to get dressed and to come out of the room with my hair covered by the robe. I wasn't in a position to argue. The guy then led me down a hallway, took me into a suite, and closed the door. Two women, who I recognized from photos as Margo and Jane MacPherson, were sitting on a couch.

I introduced myself and looked around the room. I spotted at least four listening devices. Being married to an FBI agent gives you a different perspective on things. I suggested that we sit around a table. Margo MacPherson was beside herself and wouldn't stop talking and asking questions.

"What do they want us for? Do you know? And why did they bring you here? What does an architect have to do with any of this?"

I looked at Margo and put a finger to my lips, signaling that she should shut up.

"Do you have any writing material?" I asked. "I like to jot down notes when I talk." I was speaking for the benefit of the bugs on the walls.

Margo went to a desk and gave me a yellow pad and a pen.

"This place is bugged," I wrote. "Let's be careful what we say. These people have taken over your husband's business. The reason you're here is to ensure that Angus follows their orders. They're planning a terrorist attack on five MacPherson properties next year. My guess is that I'm here so they can learn what I know about their plans. They know that my husband is an FBI agent. Excuse me, but I have to use the bathroom."

I tore off the paper from the yellow pad after Margo and Jane read it. I then walked into the bathroom, tore it up into small pieces and flushed it down the toilet. Rick would be proud of me.

"Tell us how Dad is doing," said Jane when I returned to the room.

"He's beside himself with worry, but your father is a tough man. He's holding up fine. He misses you both."

"So why are you here?" asked Jane, giving me a slow pitch so I could speak to the listening devices throughout the room.

"I don't know," I lied to the bugs. "I'm just the architect for one of Mr. MacPherson's projects. Maybe somebody didn't like my drawings," I said, introducing some lame humor into the conversation.

"It's a gorgeous design," I continued. "Angus – he insists I call him Angus – was involved in every detail. He insisted on a unique appearance, which will make these malls the most beautiful shopping centers in the country," I said, speaking to the bugs. "Each mall will be one story, with beautiful sloping steel ceilings." Of course, I didn't mention that the purpose of the ceilings was to concentrate a bomb explosion, killing thousands of people.

CHAPTER TWENTY EIGHT

"Rick, you know they're going to take you off this case," said Buster. "It's strict policy at both the CIA and the FBI that an agent with a personal involvement in a case can no longer work on it. The policy makes sense. No matter how professional a person is, when a loved one is in danger, thoughts tend to get cloudy."

"You mean I'll be taken off the case *operationally*. Don't even fucking think you're going to keep me in the dark about what's going on."

"Rick, I'm supposed to say you no longer have a need to know, but we both understand that's bullshit. I'll let you in on everything and constantly. I also need your input. You've got one of the best detective minds that I know of. We're going to need it."

⊷⊷

My phone went off. I looked at the caller ID and didn't recognize the number. I put the phone on speaker so Buster could hear. I heard what I'd been expecting.

"Mr. Bellamy, your wife is safe and is on her way to Yemen where she'll be treated well. Do not make any attempts to find her. If you do, you will not be pleased with the result. I will call you soon with our demands."

The phone went silent.

"Yemen," said Buster. "The obvious reason for that call was to throw us off. Next they'll come up with some sort of demand to make us think this is an ordinary kidnapping. The last thing they want us to think about is your theory that they'll use the MacPhersons to get information out of Ellen. Al-Qaeda combines brilliance with stupidity. But for now, let's take this as good news. They believe that *we think* that Ellen is going to Yemen."

"So let's sort this out," I said. "They've told MacPherson that his wife and daughter will be freed after Black Friday next year. Ellen came up with the theory that the shopping mall project is one big lead-up to a gigantic terror spectacular. But why would they want to release the MacPherson women? Both of them have an enormous amount of intelligence to give us. And what about Ellen, admittedly my main concern? When would they release her, and more important, *why* would they release her? We know that any ransom demand would be a bullshit attempt to throw us off. So my thinking is that they're going to kill the MacPherson women and Ellen. It's an inescapable conclusion."

Buster rubbed his forehead.

"You're right, Rick. Releasing the women would make no sense at all. The three of them can give us so much intelligence about al-Qaeda operations it would set them back years. So let's take that as a primary assumption in this operation. Ellen and the MacPherson women will be targeted for death, no matter what."

I wiped some sweat off my forehead. I noticed my hands were starting to shake.

"You could use a drink, Rick."

"No. Yes, I sure as hell could use one, but I want my mind focused. So, Mr. Spook, any thoughts on what has to be done?"

"It's obvious, Rick. We've got to get them out. The one thing we know, and they don't think we know it, is the location. I don't have to remind you that rescue operations can be dangerous, really scary. Remember Desert One, Jimmy Carter's attempt to free the Iranian hostages? A well-conceived plan, blown to shit by some bad luck. But we do have a guy inside who will feed us updates when he can. We need to start planning the rescue and wait for the right time. It would be insane for al-Qaeda to kill them before the big date next year. It would completely stop the plan in its tracks. We have time."

"Wait a minute, Buster. The MacPherson women are key to the Black Friday plan going off. What purpose does Ellen serve? She's one smart lady. I'm sure the place is bugged and that Ellen knows it. So if Ellen throws them off and gives them nothing about her knowledge of the plan, what the hell do they need her for? Killing her would help solidify their grip on Angus MacPherson's mind."

"Rick, they wouldn't harm Ellen. The MacPherson women would freak out on them."

"No, they wouldn't just shoot Ellen in front of them. They'd just tell the MacPhersons that Ellen was taken to another location. Buster, Ellen's toast. We've got to move fast."

CHAPTER TWENTY NINE

M y handler, who went by the name of Ahmed, walked into the room and told me I had to follow him. He said it was time for the MacPhersons to make a video for Angus, and our suite also served as the video studio.

"You not mention anything about Ellen Bellamy," advised Ahmed as he set up the video cam. "Tell camera that weather is beautiful in Yemen. Also say how nicely you are being treated and that your husband should not worry."

He then grabbed my arm and led me down a hallway. One of the ways I stay in shape is karate. I've even earned a black belt. If that scumbag wasn't carrying a gun, I'd have loved to get some kicking practice on his nuts. He shoved me into a small room and closed the door without even turning on a light. I groped my way along the wall until I found a light switch. When I turned it on, my eyes smarted from the sudden light. Then I noticed something in the corner under a small table. Could it be? I looked around the room, checking out every wall and the entire ceiling. There were no cameras or bugs. I walked over to the table and reached under it. There was an AK-47 with a full clip and an extra clip next to it. Obviously one of the gentlemen of the desert misplaced it. I had no plan, but I realized I had some firepower at my disposal. I opened the door to a small closet that was packed full of junk. Apparently they used the closet to hold stuff that they didn't know what to do with. I put the AK-47 behind a couple of boxes. I stepped back to make sure it wasn't visible. Now there was only one person who knew the location of the weapon, and that was me. I had no idea what I was going to do, but I had an option I didn't have a few minutes before.

After about 45 minutes, the delightful Ahmed walked into the room.

"How is you are finding light?" he inquired.

"I am finding switch by feeling along wall," (*dipshit*) I said in my finest English-Arabic.

"You are coming with me."

When we got back to the MacPherson suite, I noticed that the video cam was still on its tripod.

"You go now," he said to the MacPhersons. Another guy escorted them down the hall.

"Now you are making video for to make your husband happy. Here, read this."

He handed me a printout with my speaking lines written out.

"Do you just want me to say this, or should I talk normally to my husband?"

"Yes, read it and also be saying nice things, but nothing about where you are, and nothing about MacPherson people."

I read from my script, trying not to laugh at the skill of the screenwriter.

"I am liking Yemen much. Food is good, and weather nice. I am guest of nice peoples who are treating me with respectings. You not be worrying about anythings. I am staying in such a nice place. I hoping come see you soon, Rick."

Then I added, "I miss my dog Fiddles. Fiddles is such a good dog."

Ahmed walked back into the room and dismantled the video cam. My "message" to Rick would soon be on its way.

⊷ ⊶

Buster and I were talking when my phone buzzed, indicating I had just received a message. It showed there was an attached video. I walked over to a desk and took out my iPad – better for Buster and I to see the video.

My heart missed a beat. There was my beautiful Ellen, sitting on a stool and wearing a long black burqa, her hair totally covered.

"I am liking Yemen much. Food is good, and weather nice. I am guest of nice peoples who are treating me with respectings. You not be worrying about anythings. I am staying in such a nice place. I hoping come see you soon, Rick. I miss my dog Fiddles. Fiddles is such a good dog."

"Holy shit!" I yelled. "Ellen has an AK-47."

"Can we replay the video, Rick? I didn't catch anything about an AK-47."

"It's a code between Ellen and me. We're writing a novel together. Nothing serious, but a lot of fun. It's a crime thriller, naturally. In the draft so far, we've created an elaborate set of code phrases that the hero of the book uses to communicate with his people. 'My dog Fiddles,' means 'I have a gun.' 'Fiddles is such a good dog' means 'the gun is an AK-47.' "

"Rick, do you have a list of the codes in the book?"

"Sure, it's right after the table of contents."

I walked over to the desk and withdrew the manuscript.

"Here are all of the codes we've come up with so far."

"My God," said Buster, "there must be over a hundred. Do you think Ellen remembers most of them?"

"Ellen has a photographic memory. Besides, she dreamed up most of the codes."

"Rick, I need an electronic file of these codes to email to my man inside. I'm sure the place is bugged, but with these codes, my guy can communicate with Ellen. That means *we* can communicate with Ellen. Look at this one: 'What's for lunch,' meaning 'we'll be there in less than an hour.' Or this one: 'I'm tired,' meaning 'take cover, things are about to get hot.' Rick, this is the fucking Rosetta Stone. It's as if we have a microphone in Ellen's ear. Please copy and email this to me and I'll forward it to my guy."

Just what the hell is she going to do with an AK-47? I wondered.

CHAPTER THIRTY

B ob McLaughlin and his nephew Andrew finished their photographic safari and flew back to New York. After dropping
Andrew back in Yonkers, McLaughlin exchanged pleasantries and
swapped some stories with his brother and sister-in-law.

He continued on to Manhattan, where he was scheduled to
meet with Ali Bashara. Shit, McLaughlin thought to himself. I'm
supposed to refer to Brother Ali as Phillip Murphy, his infidel
name.

⇒ ⇐

"Peace be with you, brother Phillip."

"I've told you to knock that off, Bob. My name is Phillip Murphy,
not *brother* Phillip. And I don't want to hear 'peace be with you.'
'Hello' will do just fine."

"Sorry, Phil. I have to get used to these new rules."

McLaughlin handed a flash drive to Murphy that contained all of the photos of the nine critical electric substations across the country.

"Your next assignment, Bob, will be a pleasant one. I know you like fishing, so round up your gear and tackle. You're going to visit a few reservoirs around the country and photograph the best access spots for anyone who wants to, let's say, fish."

McLaughlin's first destination was the New Croton Reservoir in Westchester County, New York. Along with the other reservoirs he planned to visit, combined they supplied 1.2 billion gallons of drinking water to New York City every day.

CHAPTER THIRTY ONE

Watching Buster work the phone is like watching a cat eat a sardine. The man knows how to get things done, and he's got to have the world's mother lode of a contact list. Buster sat in a corner of the room with his phone in one ear and his laptop in front of him.

"Okay, good news, Rick. I've just talked to Baqir Siddiqi on a secure phone. I get nervous as hell talking to him that way, but the guy is a pro."

"Who is Baqir Siddiqi?" I asked.

"He's my guy on the inside. We call him Smitty. He's as cool an operator as they come. I emailed him the code list from your novel, and he told me that he'll memorize the codes tonight, and will start to 'talk' to Ellen tomorrow. This little game that you and Ellen played with your book could be the breakthrough we need."

Ellen and I had a lot of fun coming up with our fictional codes. Neither of us thought they might be useful to save her life someday.

"It's getting late, Buster. You should go home and hit the sack."

"I'm crashing here tonight. What did you think my bag was all about? I know you didn't invite me, so I'm inviting myself. If you wake up in the middle of the night with some revelation, I want to be here."

"Are you concerned that I shouldn't be alone?"

"Yeah, that too."

Buster's not just a good spook, he's a good friend.

⊨╪ ╪⊨

I woke up automatically at 5:30 a.m., even though I didn't sleep well. Something must be on my mind, such as my wife being violently kidnapped.

I walked into the kitchen to put on a pot of coffee. Buster (no surprise) was sitting at the table with his laptop.

"So, Mr. Action Figure, what's new since I last saw you a few hours ago?"

"Smitty has communicated with Ellen in code. It's working, Rick. Ellen said, 'Where did I leave my notebook?' meaning she sends her love. Smitty says everything is okay. He and Ellen have no problem code talking. Ellen and the MacPherson women are being treated well, and Smitty will make sure of it. I just got a message from Director Carlini. He wants to meet us at 26 Federal Plaza this morning at nine. FBI Director Watson will be there as well, along with Bennie Weinberg and Barbara Auletta. This is going to be an important meeting."

CHAPTER THIRTY TWO

A man named Baqir Siddiqi carried a tray of breakfast foods into my room after knocking on the door. I had a small apartment off the suite that I shared with the MacPhersons.

I really couldn't complain about the surroundings, but I'd just as soon blow the place up.

"I hope springtime arrives soon," said Siddiqi, in only slightly accented English.

"What? Say that again."

"I hope springtime arrives soon," ('Don't worry, help will be here soon') he repeated, staring into my eyes and smiling.

"I'm hungry as a bear," I said ('Are you on my side?').

"It looks like it's going to be a nice day," he said ('Nothing could be more true.'). A friendly little dog wagged its tail at me this morning ('Your friend says hello.')."

Holy shit. Rick's talking to me through this guy, I thought. Obviously he has the code from our novel.

"I have chores to do," said my newfound friend. ('We'll talk soon.')

So this guy must be an inside mole, somebody put there by Buster, no doubt. Like Rick said, Buster's an amazing spook. I'm actually able to communicate with my husband and the outside world. This changes everything.

I may actually live through this. But that's getting ahead of things.

CHAPTER THIRTY THREE

A car picked up Buster and me in enough time to wrestle with early Manhattan traffic. We arrived at 26 Federal Plaza at 8:55, just in time for our meeting. Bennie was already there.

We all shook hands, feeling like we were old friends. Well, I guess we were.

"Bill, please begin the meeting," said FBI Director Watson to CIA Director Carlini.

"Folks, things are starting to move incredibly fast, which is the normal speed for Buster over here. I'm going to ask Rick and Buster to bring us up to date on what's going on. Buster briefed me already, but I want everyone to hear it."

Buster and I gave a play-by-play of the previous two days, starting with Ellen's kidnapping. We told them about the code Ellen and I had developed, and Buster discussed Smitty's involvement on the inside, although he wouldn't mention his name, either in English or Arabic.

After we were done, Sarah Watson turned to me and said, "Rick, I'm sure you understand that I have to relieve you of any operational management of this case. It's a standard policy. If an agent has a family member who's been compromised, not to mention kidnapped, you can't serve on the case."

I was about to speak when Buster chimed in.

"Madam Director, if I may. Rick and I discussed this last night, and I believe Rick fully understands, although he'll speak for himself. But I can't suggest more strongly that we put a limit *only* on Rick's operational involvement. We need him on the inside with us. If Rick hadn't told me about the code he and Ellen came up with for their book, we'd all be standing around with our heads up our asses, if you pardon my bluntness."

"I couldn't agree more, Buster," said Watson. "If guns come out, Rick stays put. Other than that, he's still on the case. So now we have to turn our minds to exactly what we're going to do. Bill (turning to Carlini), do you agree that this is what we're up to this morning?"

"Yes, Sarah, I agree. I'd like to hear Buster's opinion."

"It really isn't complicated," said Buster. "We have to attack and hit them fast and hard. As I told you, I've got a guy on the inside, a good guy. Rick convinced me that if we just sit and wait, his wife Ellen and the MacPherson women will be killed. We can't come up with any reason al-Qaeda would want them to live. They may keep the MacPherson women alive until after the Black Friday operation, but then they're not only worthless to al-Qaeda, they're a big security risk for them. We can't figure out any use Ellen may be to them once they've gotten all the information from her that they can. Unless we want to see these three women killed, it's time to lock and load."

"Assess the level of danger for us, Buster."

"It will be dangerous but doable. Attacking a hostage location is always a tricky operation. We've had the place under surveillance for two days, and we have satellite reconnaissance and a 24-hour video recorder in a van up the street. We've identified ten men, counting my guy, which means we have nine people to worry about. In her video, Ellen indicated to Rick, in code of course, that she has access to an AK-47. I think a dozen FBI SWAT team guys in the middle of the night should do the trick. My guy can communicate with Ellen to let her and the MacPhersons know when to lay low. We know exactly where they are in the house, so we know where we have to avoid shooting. Ellen can keep her AK-47 trained on the door to the suite she shares with the MacPhersons. The SWAT guys will have a code to identify themselves."

"Does Ellen know how to use an AK-47, Rick?" asked Sarah Watson.

"Yes, Madam Director. After I convinced Ellen to get a pistol permit, I insisted she get checked out on an assault weapon. I gave her some intensive training. She's also a black belt in karate. My pretty, feminine wife is one tough lady."

But she's not bullet proof, I thought.

"I'll get in touch with our local SWAT team immediately," said Watson.

"We'll meet back here in two days," said Carlini. "Is that okay with you Sarah?"

"As Buster said, Bill, it's time to lock and load."

The morning's meeting did nothing for my nerves. We were actively planning a shootout at the house where Ellen was a hostage. I agreed that it was the only choice, but that did nothing for the knot in my stomach, a knot that reminded me that the woman I love would soon be in danger of her life.

CHAPTER THIRTY FOUR

I looked at the caller ID on my cell phone. I didn't recognize the number, so I expected it would be one of Ellen's captors with another message. A heavy Scottish brogue greeted me on the other end.

"Good afternoon, lad. It's Angus MacPherson. It appears you and I share a bond that we wish we didn't. Would you please meet me at my house this afternoon at three?"

My rental car pulled under the *porte cachere* at the back of the mansion. Angus MacPherson was waiting for me in the doorway.

I walked up the two steps and extended my hand. He grabbed me around the neck and gave me a bear hug.

"Welcome to the brotherhood of kidnap victims, lad."

"I wish neither of us belonged to that group, Angus. I hope our membership will lapse sooner than later."

He led me into the den and poured two tumblers of brandy.

"So have they contacted you, Rick?"

"Yes. Take a look at this video I got yesterday." I showed him my iPad, with Ellen reciting her lines.

"I am liking Yemen much. Food is good, and weather nice. I am guest of nice peoples who are treating me with respectings. You not be worrying about anythings. I am staying in such a nice place. I hoping come see you soon, Rick. I miss my dog Fiddles. Fiddles is such a good dog."

"It's obvious, lad, that Ellen didn't write the lines herself," said Angus with a chuckle. "So she misses her dog as well as you."

"Uh, yes." I wasn't about to let Angus know that she was speaking in our private code.

"Margo and Jane are in Yemen, too," said Angus. "Or so I've been told."

"Well, the only thing we have to go on is what we're told, right?"

"Do you really have a dog named Fiddles?"

"Why do you ask?"

"Let us be frank with each other, Rick. I have my sources, good sources. Even though I don't control my security company any more, I still keep some of my best people, former employees, on my personal payroll. So tell me, do you really believe they're in Yemen? Or could it be much closer, perhaps as close as New Jersey?"

"Angus, you asked me to be frank, and I will. There are things that you don't know, and things that you shouldn't know. In the FBI, we have a doctrine that we follow called a 'need to know.' It has nothing to do with a person's trustworthiness, and God knows we trust you. But there are some matters that that only a few people should have access to. Leave this up to us, to the FBI and the CIA."

"So it is New Jersey, then. Tenafly to be exact?"

"Angus, I don't know how you came across that information, but please leave this to us. We know what we're doing and how to do it."

"Rick, I asked you to come here for a reason. Let me share my thinking with you. I have no reason to believe that Margo and Jane are in danger until the day after Black Friday. After that I believe they will be killed. But your lovely wife, on the other hand is more expendable, shall we say. You may be ahead of me on this, but I think that the only reason they kidnapped Ellen was to open a conversation with Margo. They want to find out what Ellen knows. Once that is accomplished, they have no reason to keep the poor lass alive."

"We're on the same page, Angus. All I can tell you is that we're aware of the situation, and we're planning to, well, intervene. That's all I can tell you."

"Let me show you a video that I received this morning, Rick."

He waved me over to his desk and turned on the computer monitor to play the morning's video. Margo and Jane MacPherson appeared on the screen.

"Hello, Angus. Jane and I are well. They are treating us gently. We're enjoying the sunshine. I always enjoy sunshine, especially here in beautiful Yemen. We're going to say goodbye for now. Hope to talk to you soon. We love you."

"Is there something in that message that I missed, Angus?"

"Rick, a man in my position always worries about kidnapping. My advisors have always counseled me that Margo and I should have a code, a way we could communicate even if one of us can't talk openly. You just heard Margo say that she 'always enjoys sunshine.' It means 'there is danger.' Sort of like Ellen talking about Fiddles. I know you don't own a dog. Ellen was communicating with you by code. Am I correct?"

It was suddenly clear to me that I had to bring MacPherson inside. He had a need to know because *I* needed to know what *he* knew.

"Yes, Angus, it's a code. Ellen and I invented it for a crime novel we're writing together. When she talked about Fiddles, she was saying that she has a gun. When she said that he is a good dog, she meant that it's an AK-47. But you just said that Margo was signaling that they're in danger."

"No, lad. She didn't say that *they* were in danger, just that there *was* danger. I believe she was referring to Ellen. Rick, I hope you people are keeping a close watch on that house in Tenafly."

"Yes, Angus, the house is being watched closely, more than closely. As I mentioned, we're planning an intervention. It could be dangerous – hell, it *will* be dangerous. I'm deeply inside this mission, but I have no operational role because of Ellen. But trust me, my friend, I have a lot to say, and I have a big stake in this just like you."

"Rick, has anybody figured out what these bastards want?"

"Yes, Angus. Ellen figured it out. She met with an engineering professor friend at West Point. The whole idea behind those sloping stainless steel ceilings on your buildings is to kill people. Ellen called them blast concentrators, designed to maximize the effect of a bomb explosion. All human beings in any of the malls will be killed instantly by simultaneous bomb detonations."

"Dear God, lad. I expect at least 75,000 people at all of the malls at any given time on that day. And those bastards call *us* heathens. When did you say you're planning the intervention?"

"All I can say, Angus, is that it will be soon, as soon as possible. I promise I'll call you as soon as the operation starts."

CHAPTER THIRTY FIVE

Baqir Siddiqi, my newfound friend, entered our suite and knocked on the door to my apartment.

"Mrs. Bellamy," he said, "it is time for the MacPhersons to record a video message. You must now come with me now," he said, speaking sternly for the benefit of the bugs on the walls.

He led me, just like the last time, to the small room down the hall. He gestured to me to enter the room and closed the door behind me. I realized that I suddenly had an opportunity that may not show up again. The AK-47 that I stashed in the closet wouldn't do me any good if the shit hit the fan while I was in my apartment. I had to move the gun, and I had the opportunity to do it.

Thank God that Siddiqi was my handler that day.

One of the good things about a burqa, well maybe the only good thing about a burqa, is that you can conceal a lot under it. As soon as Siddiqi closed the door, I walked over to the closet. I closed my eyes and took a deep breath, hoping I'd find the gun where I hid it. There it was, right where I left it, along with the extra clip.

I wore slacks under my burqa, so I loosened the belt and slipped the strap of the gun under it. I looked into a mirror. Just a lady in a burqa, with no bulge showing.

A few minutes later, there was a knock on the door. Siddiqi opened it and said, "Another friendly little dog wagged his tail at me." (Our code for "your friend says hello.")

It was weird communicating with Rick through code, but if that's what it took I'd settle for it.

Siddiqi led me back to the suite and started to leave.

"Will I be making a video today?" I asked. No need for code, just a simple question.

"No, tomorrow maybe," said Siddiqi brusquely.

After he left, I walked into my apartment and went for the closet. My wardrobe consisted of another burqa. I guess they figured I would like an occasional change of wardrobe, from black to black. I lifted the hanger and slung the strap of the gun around it, and then covered the strap with a fold from the burqa. I placed the extra ammunition clip under a box on the floor.

I had no idea what I would do with the gun, but I felt comfortable having it closer.

I was having a hard time believing what was going on. Being kidnapped was the most frightening thing that ever happened to me, but now that I was in the custody of these slimeballs, my mind constantly wandered back and forth about what I was supposed to do. Siddiqi, my code-talking friend, made things a little easier. He told me that help would be on the way. But when, and what would it look like? And what the hell was I supposed to do, just hide under the bed? That's not my nature. Okay, time to stop this crap, I thought. Siddiqi was obviously a skilled agent and knew what he was doing.

I missed Rick. I missed him like crazy. I hoped I'd live to see him again.

CHAPTER THIRTY SIX

"Rick," said Buster, "I'd like to introduce you to my good friend, Lieutenant Leo Burton, formerly with of the US Navy SEALs, and now commander of the New York FBI Enhanced SWAT team."

"Pleasure to meet you, Rick. Please call me Leo."

"In technical terms," Buster said, "Leo is what is known as an ass kicker. We've worked operations together in the past, and I couldn't be happier to have him involved. Leo's going to lead the unit that attacks the safe house."

I winced at the word attack, but I knew that's exactly what it would be.

"Can I just get something out of the way first, guys?" said Leo.

"Rick, I understand your wife is one of the hostages. I'm concerned about your involvement in this mission. Simply stated, an aching heart can fuck with your head."

"Don't worry, Leo. I won't have any operational involvement. That's from orders on high. But I can help you with the planning and that's what I'm here for."

"Buster's updated me on what we know about the house and the personnel involved," said Leo. "To be honest with you guys, any hostage situation is dangerous. Don't worry, SWAT teams train for every operation as if it's impossible, but we have a few things going for us in this one. First, Buster managed to get a man inside. I can't tell you how much that will help. I also understand that Smitty, our inside guy, can communicate with your wife in code. That's another plus, a big plus. Few hostage situations allow for inside communication. Also, Buster tells me we have nine bad guys to worry about. I've seen odds a lot worse than that. Just before we launch the operation, Smitty will place cameras on the walls all over the place. That will give us a big jump on knowing where to go."

"Leo," I said, "I guess Buster told you that Ellen has access to a gun, an AK-47 no less. I don't want her involved in a shootout, not that I have anything to say about it, but just be aware that Ellen is a smart, levelheaded woman. She also has guts. I mention this because I'm sure that she'll be ready to protect herself and the MacPherson women."

"Is you wife experienced in handling an AK-47?

"Yes, I trained her myself. She's a damn accurate shot, although with an assault rifle, just knowing how to use it is more important than accuracy. But you can count on Ellen to make the right decisions."

"I want to avoid that," said Leo, "but it's good to know the capability is there. I won't minimize this, Rick. Anything, and I mean *anything*, can go wrong in a hostage situation."

CHAPTER THIRTY SEVEN

Tony Lombardo and George Rendell met as planned at the Morton Flying School in Phoenix, Arizona. They were early and the school had not yet opened.

"Peace be upon you, Brother Gamal," said Lombardo.

"Hey, Tony, cut that crap out. Remember that Ali Bashara, I mean Phil Murphy, said we're not to greet each other that way."

"I'm still trying to adjust to the new rules. Thanks for reminding me."

"So how are you feeling about your flying skills, George?"

"I'm getting better with each lesson. Soon my skills will be used for the glory of Allah."

"Fucking George, you're not supposed to say that."

"Sorry, I'm getting as bad as you. And you don't have to call me fucking George."

"Stop fucking up and I'll stop calling you that."

"So what do you think our assignment will be, Tony?"

"We won't know until shortly before the mission, whatever the mission will be. But I overheard Bashara…, I mean Murphy's assistant, saying we needed to be ready soon."

CHAPTER THIRTY EIGHT

My code-talking friend Siddiqi told me that the attack would come at night. He suggested that I try to sleep as much as possible during the day and stay awake at night. If Siddiqi wasn't there, I'd have been scared out of my mind. I was scared out of my mind anyway.

I hung my extra burqa over the window to block as much light as possible so I could sleep, but not before transferring my AK-47 to the underside of my mattress.

Rick had done a great job training me to handle guns, and I developed an accurate shot with a pistol. Rick praised me, of course, but the shooting range officer told me I was one of the best students he'd seen in years. But shooting a gun and shooting it at another human being are two different things. Besides, I didn't have a pistol, but an AK-47. Rick trained me on that as well, but it's the same as with a pistol: shooting it is one thing, being in a gunfight is another.

A few days ago, I was a diligent architect, minding my own business and working at a drafting table. Then I uncovered a terrorist plot, blew the whistle to my husband and his colleagues, and managed to get myself kidnapped by a bunch of jihadis.

It was 3 p.m. and I was trying to sleep. Siddiqi had a great idea about staying up at night. When and if the late night shooting started, I didn't want to be yawning and stretching.

If I live through this, I'm going to convince Rick that we need to write another novel, not to mention take a long vacation.

If I live through this.

CHAPTER THIRTY NINE

B uster, Lt. Leo, and I continued our meeting after a short lunch break.

"Okay, guys, let's take a look at the safe house," said Lt. Leo as he laid out photos on the table. "The jihadis were smart to pick this house. As you can see, it's up on a hill, which slopes off on all four sides. Here is a night photo. Notice the bright security lights surrounding the place. Any assault under the conditions you're looking at means running uphill in a bright light, not my idea of a good way to launch an attack. I've communicated with Buster's guy Smitty, and he'll hit the lights just before we go. We'll attack at 2 a.m., when most of the occupants will be asleep. Surprise is always the best way to attack, and that's exactly what we're looking for. Smitty's armed, and he'll take out the guards. He'll alert Ellen just before we storm the place, and she'll keep her gun trained on the door to the suite. What's missing is a dark staging area. I'm thinking we'll have my guys dropped off a couple of blocks away, and I'll give the order to go as soon as Smitty turns off the lights. It's going to be tricky as hell. The road in front of the house is well travelled and there are street lights every 50 feet."

Buster's phone rang. He walked out of the office to answer it. He came back within five minutes, looking like he just won the lottery.

"Our staging problems are over," said Buster. "The guy on the phone was a man named Mark Drury. He's a former Marine colonel. After he retired, he started a second career with the Newark Police Department, where he most recently served as chief of detectives. And the most important thing is that he lives right next door to the safe house. He's a widower and lives alone in a big house, and is more than happy to let us use his place as a staging area for the attack. I've been waiting for his call. He had to cancel some plans to help us out."

"Did you have to let him know the details of the operation?" I asked.

"Of course, and I'm not worried about it. I didn't tell him that Ellen and the MacPherson women are the hostages, only that it's a hostage situation. The guy is like a kid who just got a pony for Christmas. He's 70 years old and has been away from the action for a long time. When he was with the Marines he commanded a recon company in Vietnam. So we have a friendly combat veteran who also was in law enforcement. This guy is a gift from heaven."

"How did you find him?" I asked.

"I checked the real estate records to see who the neighbors were. Just basic cop work. I researched Drury out and discovered his credentials. So I called him and introduced myself."

"What was his reaction?"

"He began by asking me one question, 'Is this about those scumbags next door?' This guy has been aboard our mission before he even knew about it. He told me the lights shine constantly at all hours of the night. He also said that different cars come and go all the time. And get this, he was good friends with the former owner of the safe house. It was designed by the same architect as his house. So he contacted the architect and obtained the plans, which he's going to happily share with us. So, guys, we have Smitty inside, a tough hombre next door, and detailed room plans."

"I've worked on a lot tougher house invasions than this," said Leo. "But I remind you that this is a hostage operation. Anything can go wrong."

"When do you think it will happen?" I asked.

"We'll be good to go in less than a week."

"Do you see anything that could slow us down?" asked Buster.

"Yes. Snow. It's the only thing that could force a delay. As former SEALs, our guys own the night, but that assumes darkness. I can't have my guys silhouetted against a white landscape making themselves targets. Even with the flood lights out, snow would be a problem."

"Shit," said Buster, "even though it's only mid-December, the forecasters are talking about a possible heavy snowstorm next week, followed by unseasonably cold weather, which means it won't melt any time soon."

"Bottom line," said Leo, "if it snows we'll have to be patient. It's the only thing that could screw up the operation. If we catch a break, I see next Wednesday night as an ideal time. There will be no moon, so we'll have plenty of darkness, again, assuming no snow. And from what Buster just said, that could be a doubtful assumption."

⊷⊶

Buster, Leo, and I drove in a rental car to Colonel Drury's house in Tenafly. The colonel told us to drive up the north side of the house, which is completely obscured from the target house. It was

7:30 p.m. We wanted to arrive in darkness so we could assess the conditions for the night of the raid. I was having a hard time coming to grips with the fact that I was only a couple of hundred feet from Ellen and there was nothing I could do about it.

Colonel Drury was a big man, about 6'2" and 225 pounds. Buster's description of him as a little kid who just got a pony was right on. The colonel looked happy to be in action again. He even wore his old combat fatigues, which fit him a bit snugly. He walked us through a den over to a window that faced the safe house. It was next to a door leading in that direction. The window had a light curtain over it and we couldn't be seen from the target house.

"Lieutenant Burton, I hope you don't mind input from an old Marine, but I have a couple of suggestions about how you and your men may want to proceed."

"Colonel, the day I don't listen to a recon Marine is the day I hang up my badge. Please tell us what you have in mind."

"As you can see, those fucking security lights make this house look like an outdoor circus. That path in front of you is the quickest access to the house, but the bright lights would make you all easy targets."

Buster told him about Smitty and the plan to have him kill the lights on cue. The colonel gave Buster a thumbs up.

Colonel Drury then walked over to a desk and withdrew a portfolio from the top drawer.

"I know you've been waiting for this. Here are the architectural plans for the house, including detailed room plans. My late wife and I were good friends with the previous owners and we spent a lot of time in their house. I can tell you that the rooms look exactly like these 30-year-old drawings, except for about four feet added onto the kitchen." He marked the addition in red.

He then took out a top view plan of the house.

"Buster, I assume you have a satellite photo of the house as it looks now."

Buster took out a few satellite photos and spread them on the desk.

"Great," said the colonel. He looked at Leo.

"I'm going to make a couple of suggestions, Lieutenant. You guys know what the hell you're doing, so most of my input will be as a homeowner, a homeowner who's a combat veteran. I recommend you post snipers here, here, and here," he said, putting small circles on the photo. "This foliage is all evergreen so it will provide excellent cover. You may also want to post a couple of your men on the third floor of my house. There's an outside terrace area, excellent for viewing the house next door and also great for sniping. See that tool shed next to the house? Good spot to take before you launch your final assault."

"Colonel, is it okay with you if we put video cameras at a few locations on the third floor?" asked Lt. Leo.

"Sure. I've already shot a bunch of stills. Whatever you need, just let me know. My house has eight bedrooms and nine bathrooms, so we can fit your entire unit."

"Colonel, I hope you understand that I have a substantial budget for this kind of operation, so you'll be well-compensated for your hospitality," said Buster.

The colonel waved him off.

"Make out the check to The Wounded Warrior Project. Consider me one of your troops."

"If it's okay with you, sir, I'd like to start bringing my men tomorrow. I don't want to call attention to a bunch of people showing up at your house at one time."

"I'll go you one better, lieutenant. Tell me where to pick them up and I'll drive them here in groups in my car. I'll pull right into the garage, and nobody will notice a thing."

"You'd make a great spook, colonel," said Buster.

"Okay," said Lt. Leo, "*Operation Betsy* is now under way."

"I know that operation names don't mean anything, but how did you come up with that one?" asked the colonel.

"It's the name of the cat I had as a kid," said Buster.

"Gentlemen, let's make Buster's little kitty proud," said the colonel.

CHAPTER FORTY

Angus MacPherson stood next to a bulldozer in Tucson, Arizona, the site of the first of five planned shopping malls. Photographers and reporters from local newspapers crowded the scene to memorialize the occasion. Carmella McGrath, Mayor of Tucson, was also on hand for the ribbon cutting.

"Ladies and gentlemen," said the Mayor, as cameras clicked, "we're here on a wonderful occasion. With all of the horrible violence of the past few weeks, we can take pride that our city is on the move – a move of peace and prosperity.

"Our country has terrible enemies, but today we can enjoy a new future for Tucson, a future brought to us by our good friend Angus MacPherson. This beautiful new shopping center will mean jobs, jobs, and more jobs."

And a body count that you won't believe, thought MacPherson.

"Mr. MacPherson, give us a smile," said one of the photographers.

MacPherson managed a tight grin. So with or without Ellen Bellamy, the construction plans moved forward. MacPherson had his mind on another plan, not in Arizona but in Tenafly, New

Jersey. He could think of little else since his meeting with Rick Bellamy.

He looked beyond the reporters and photographers at a man standing on the edge of the crowd. The man was one of his al-Qaeda handlers. MacPherson closed his eyes and imagined shooting the bastard.

That afternoon, the President of the United States would give a speech that would change history.

CHAPTER FORTY ONE

CIA Director Bill Carlini was in New York at 26 Federal Plaza to meet with us. At 11:45 a.m., he walked to the head of the table. It was Saturday morning. Recent events had scratched the idea of taking weekends off. The subject of *Operation Betsy* and the soon-to-begin rescue of Ellen and the MacPherson women was not on the table. The operation was so sensitive that Carlini didn't want to discuss it in the open. The others at the meeting included General Dwight Simon, Chairman of the Joint Chiefs of Staff, and FBI Director Sarah Watson.

"Before we begin our meeting," said Director Carlini, "we'll listen to President Reynolds who is about to address the nation." He clicked the remote at the TV. "I think this will be one of the most important speeches he's ever given."

The President walked up to the podium.

"My fellow Americans. I speak to you today, not as a man who has all the answers, but as the man you elected to lead our great nation. The events of the past few weeks are the culmination of evil itself. There's no way to sugar coat it, and I won't. Our nation, indeed the freedom-loving world, is under attack from a faceless enemy, an enemy that doesn't answer to any government, an enemy that has nothing to negotiate, an enemy that is dedicated to one goal – the destruction of our way of life. I'm not going to lie to you and say that we are faced with a perversion of a religion. We're faced with perversion itself, a perversion that wears a mask of religion, but it's only a mask."

He cleared his throat and took a sip of water. The man looked, well there's only one way to put it, the President looked nervous.

"World War III has begun," Reynolds continued. He paused, looking straight at the camera. He said nothing for 30 seconds. "You heard me right. The world is at war. It's not any kind of war that we've ever seen before. It's not a war that was declared by a nation state. It's a war that has been declared by evil men who desire to kill in large numbers. It's a war that makes no sense, a war that is carried out against innocent civilian men, women, and children. It's a war that knows no boundaries, waged by an enemy that doesn't recognize the Geneva Convention or any other form of civilized behavior."

He took another sip of water, something he seldom does.

"Is this a war that will end? Will there be a day when we sit down with enemy leadership and sign a document? The answer to both of those questions is no. There will never be an Armistice Day holiday to celebrate the end of World War III because the enemy has no single source of leadership. The war will end when the enemy decides to embrace humanity, not to kill indiscriminately. But in the meantime, we will fight this war. With our allies all over the world, we will fight to preserve human freedom and dignity. We will fight to keep the enemy off guard, and strike at its heart. God Bless America."

Our meeting room was as silent as a mountaintop. We just heard a shocking speech, a speech that was obviously written with one goal – to level with the American people, and the people of the world.

Carlini turned off the TV and walked to the head of the table.

Whenever I saw Carlini talk, I was impressed with the guy's cool leadership. His job consisted of managing one crisis after another. He always did so with a calmness that I found inspiring. But this morning, Carlini didn't look his usual smooth self. He looked shaken, just like the President.

"You've just heard the President say what a lot of us have thought for a long time. World War III has begun."

Carlini let his words linger. He didn't follow up with an immediate explanation or ask for input. The President just announced something that hit us like an explosion. I looked at General Simon, Chairman of the Joint Chiefs, the country's top operational military man. He looked at Carlini and nodded in agreement. Carlini looked at Sarah Watson and simply said, "Sarah?" inviting her comments.

"I agree with the President's assessment," said Watson. "He's our Commander in Chief, so I have no option but to agree. We've met with the White House staff, as well as General Simon here. It's an inescapable conclusion. The West is at war, an undeclared war. The reason the war is undeclared is because there is no nation to declare it. Of course ISIS calls itself a state, an Islamic State, but it isn't a country in any historical sense. No, this war has been declared by a vast network, and I do mean vast. The network, as we all know too well, consists of radical jihadists the world over. Since the attacks of 10/15 and the sinking of the two cruise ships, we've concluded that we have to be on a war footing. Gone are the days when a suicide bombing in a crowded bazaar in the Middle East is front-page news. Sure, we'll still read about those incidents, but we're now involved in something much bigger. After the attacks of 9/11, the radicals avoided direct assaults on the American homeland. That all changed on 10/15. We're now under attack in a way that we've never imagined." She looked at Carlini.

"I'd like to hear your thoughts, Buster," said Carlini.

"There's only one possible solution," said Buster. "We have to infiltrate. It's going to take an army of operatives, far more than we've ever used before. Al-Qaeda and ISIS have figured out that they have to lay low and conceal their identity. We're seeing less proselytizing and open recruiting. Traffic on radical websites has slowed to a trickle. They have figured out that we can track the visitors, and they're lurking in the shadows. Our database is being choked off. We need to feed it information or else the list of terror suspects will be worthless. I hate to say this, but we're going to need a gigantic network of observers watching, listening, and reporting. The only way this war will ever end will come from within Islam, from religious leaders who decide it's time to take a stance. Until then, our country will be a very different place to live. I think the President just teed up that ball."

"Buster, have you begun recruiting operatives?" asked Carlini.

"Yes, sir, and it sickens me, but it's what we have to do. We've got to feed information to the database because our usual way of gathering facts just doesn't work. The only thing that will stop this country from being run like the Gestapo is careful oversight from the Senate Intelligence Committee. As a spy, I hate being questioned, but as an American I welcome it."

"Director Carlini," said a loud voice over the intercom. "I suggest you turn on the television, sir."

⇥⊹ ⊹⇤

Everyone in the room let out an expletive. Some groaned. Some said, "Now what?" Some just said, "Oh, shit."

"This is Wolf Blitzer reporting for CNN. We have just gotten word that a bomb has exploded in the Bryant-Denny Stadium

where the game between Alabama and Notre Dame had just begun. The bomb went off behind the Notre Dame bench on the
fifty-yard line. We have a live video feed, but the scene is too grisly
to show our audience without editing. What I can tell you is that
the view is one of utter devastation. Bodies were flung hundreds of
feet, and a large section of the stadium seats is gone. It had to be a
large bomb to cause such a gigantic explosion. We go now to Sam
Tillery, a reporter with our CNN affiliate in Tuscaloosa."

"Wolf, the scene here is utter chaos. I'm looking at the site of
the blast from the broadcast booth, and to say that it's sickening
would be an understatement. Besides the bomb blast, the violence
continues right before my eyes. Panic has gripped the crowd, and
the exits are choked with people stampeding, trying to escape. It's
too early to report deaths or injuries, but I can tell you from what
I'm looking at, the death toll will be high. And it will continue to
mount as the panic spreads."

"Sam, excuse me but I'm getting a report of another breaking
story," said Blitzer.

Blitzer paused while holding his right hand to his earpiece.
Despite his television makeup, his face looked pale.

"Ladies and gentlemen, I've just received a report that there
has been another explosion at a college football game. Florida
State was about to kick off to Oklahoma at *Doak Campbell Stadium* in
Tallahassee, Florida, when a bomb exploded in the restaurant
overlooking the field. The restaurant, which holds 450 people, col-
lapsed and fell onto the seats below. We haven't gotten a report
of injuries or deaths, but the stadium is absolutely chaotic. The
first responders are being overwhelmed by the panicked crowd.
This explosion occurred two minutes after the terrorist attack on
Bryant-Denny Stadium in Alabama."

Blitzer, normally a seasoned pro, looked like he was about to
throw up.

⇒⊹⊹⇐

"Notice that Blitzer used the words terrorist attack," said Watson. "Nobody doubts what we're up against."

"Folks," said Blitzer. "We've just heard the President of the United States inform us that World War III has begun."

Blitzer looked down. He seemed to be groping for his next sentence.

"At this time a lot of people are asking a question," said Blitzer. "Is there anyone in the Muslim community who wants to stop the killing? Any one at all?"

CHAPTER FORTY TWO

"Rick, it's Buster. Please come to my office. I just got a call from a guy I want you to meet.

I'll tell you about him when you get here. I also called Bennie. You'll see why."

Bennie Weinberg and I walked into Buster's office. His normally immaculate desk was piled high with papers.

"Let's go into the conference room," Buster said. "The guy will be here in about 20 minutes. This could be bullshit, which is why I asked Bennie to be here. The man's name is Muhammed Bushariff. He's a Muslim cleric and the imam of a mosque in Brooklyn."

"Is he from the Middle East, or is he one of the homegrown types we've been talking about?" I asked.

"He was born and raised in Brooklyn, but both of his parents immigrated from Saudi Arabia. He speaks English without an accent, just a hint of Brooklynese. I met him a couple of times on different investigations. He's one of the few clerics who would give us any assistance at all. He's always been polite and quite helpful on occasion. One time he even called me to volunteer some information about a guy on our watch list. I sometimes get the feeling that Bushariff would like to change careers. There's nothing about him that could be described as radical."

"Can we trust him?" I asked.

"Hey, that's our job to decide. In this room, we have an FBI agent, a shrink, and a spook. If we can't figure out if he's for real, who can?"

Buster's assistant knocked on the door. "Mr. Bushariff is here to see you."

Our guest walked in. Bushariff was a thin man about 5'11" with a medium length beard. He wore a conservative suit, not Muslim garb, except for a taqiyah on his head. Buster introduced us and we all shook hands. I noticed the guy had a firm grip and looked me right in the eyes when he shook my hand.

We sat around the conference table. Buster asked Bushariff to sit at the head. Buster has a keen sense of protocol, and he figured it would be polite to give Bushariff a prominent spot at the table.

"So, Muhammed, what would you like to talk to us about?" asked Buster.

He took off his taqiyah and threw it on the table.

"I've had it," he said loudly. "I've fucking had it."

I'd met a lot of Muslim clerics over the years, but this was the first time I heard one launch an f-bomb. Bushariff took a deep breath and expelled it with force.

"I've been going through a religious crisis for some time. I was born a Muslim and raised a Muslim, and never questioned it. It was my faith. Whenever there was a radical Muslim terrorist act, I would always say a few words at the mosque, things like, 'this is not our way,' or 'some of our brothers have strayed from the path of righteousness, but ours is the path of peace.' Shit like that. What I wanted to say was, 'Who are these crazy fucking people?' Like all Muslim clerics, one of my jobs is to do PR for the faith. When was the last time you heard a cleric denounce terrorism like he meant it? Your typical imam, and I hate to say it because I've done this myself, would say something like, 'we denounce terrorism *but*, we also denounce the terror committed against Muslims.' Always a fucking *but*. When the Twin Towers came down, you heard constant bullshit about how bad it was, but – always the *but* – the men who did this were provoked by injustice, blah, blah, blah. It started to dawn on me that I'm a human being, an American, and I unwittingly share membership in a club full of savage animals."

Muhammed stopped and took a deep breath. He looked like he wanted to put his fist through a wall. This guy was really worked up. He was genuinely pissed.

"Muhammed," said Buster.

"Call me Mike."

"Okay, Mike, are there many more like you who share your discontent with terrorism?"

"Not nearly enough, Buster. Hey, look at the numbers. Estimates vary all over the place, but I've read the polls and so have you. It's scary. If only one percent of Muslims worldwide are radical, that translates into 15 million people. I read a Pew Research poll taken in 2013, which found that 19 percent of Muslim Americans believe suicide bombings in defense of Islam are at least partially justified. That's almost a fifth of American Muslims. The global average is 28 percent in the countries they surveyed. I mean, holy shit, a lot of people out there are okay with the bombings of the past few weeks. The college football game bombings on Saturday finally put me over the edge. My daughter is good friends with the sister of the Notre Dame quarterback. That poor kid's body got blown all over the fifty-yard line."

"Mike," said Bennie, "my wife is a college professor and an expert on the Middle East. She tells me that even she can't figure out what the hell is going on. Do you have an opinion why the West is so hated?"

"Well, look at it this way, Doctor Ben. Remember that study done the year after 9/11 about Arab countries. The people on the study commission were 100 percent Arab, so the report can't be accused of bias. The report found that in 700 years, the number of books translated into Arabic in all Muslim countries combined was less than the number of translations in Spain in *one year*, and Spain is the smallest country in Europe. Ignorance is bad enough, but when you have millions of people who are content to live in the dark, they'll listen to anything."

"And yet you're still a Muslim?" said Bennie.

"In name only. My faith has been shattered by the non-stop killings. The past few weeks have fucking cemented it. If I said that in some circles I'd have my head chopped off."

"Mike," said Buster, "are you aware of any developments concerning what we call 'homegrown' jihadis, people who are otherwise Western but have converted to radical Islam?"

"Yes. I've talked about this with some other imams, guys I think I can trust. All of a sudden, I noticed that these 'homegrown' types weren't showing up at the mosque. My friends confirmed it. Then I met a guy who I knew as Ali. I said the usual to him, 'peace be with you brother Ali.' He immediately corrected me and said that I should call him Bill, and that his last name was Jackson. I asked him why and he said something I'll never forget. He said, 'Jihad is best waged from the shadows. I want to be invisible to the infidels.' These fucking people are hiding from you, Buster."

"Mike," I said, "can you help us?"

"Yes, that's what I'm here for."

He handed me a list of names.

"These are men who used to worship at my mosque. They're all what you call 'homegrown.' And here is a list of names given to me by other imams. I didn't jot them down but memorized the names when they told me about them. Looking over my shoulder has become a regular form of exercise for me."

"I suggest that you be cautious, Mike," said Buster, "very cautious. Please, just act normal. If, or I should say, when, there is another terror attack, just issue your standard mild denunciation."

"You don't have to worry about that, Buster. Remember those newspaper reports a couple of years ago about Ahmed Muzir, an imam in Michigan. He went on a tirade, furiously denouncing terrorism from his pulpit. That guy had a pair of brass balls. He was also killed, beheaded after a sermon. I want to help in any way I can. But I'd like to keep my head attached to my neck if at all possible."

"Mike," said Buster, "I can't tell you how important this is for our country. Welcome to the modern world, my fellow patriot."

"As I said at the start of this meeting, Buster, I've fucking had it."

⚔

After Bushariff left, we stayed in the conference room to debrief the meeting with our new friend.

"Well, Bennie," I said, "did our guest make it past your bullshit detector okay?"

"The guy's for real. He's one of those people who suddenly got enlightened and had an epiphany. I think we have an important player on our side. All he has to do is keep his ears and eyes open, and tip us off when he learns something."

"And keeping our new friend Mike from getting whacked is a high priority," I said.

"Yes, and let's move carefully," said Buster. "He seems honestly passionate about helping us, but he's not a trained spy. I'd like to use him to feed our database with information from around the country. Like you, Rick, I don't want to see this guy's passion get him into trouble. He's too valuable. He's also a good guy. Let's hope that Mike can lead us to some more Mikes."

"I wonder if he knows anything about the safe house in Tenafly," I said.

"I doubt it," said Buster. "Imam Mike is an observer, not a management insider."

CHAPTER FORTY THREE

Siddiqi knocked on my door.

"Madam Bellamy, it's time for another video message."

Siddiqi was nothing if not polite. I guessed it was because he was on our side.

"I wonder when the temperature will get warmer," he said, code for, 'the time will come soon.'

I supposed that should have made me happy, but it gave me a knot in my stomach. Things would soon get violent, and the closest I ever came to combat was when I kicked a nasty little dog that tried to bite my ankle.

Siddiqi led me down the hallway to the small room where I had found the gun. It seemed the jihadi production company decided to use that room as the new studio for making our videos. The room, I noticed last time, had no listening or viewing devices on the walls or the ceiling. It was bug free as best I could tell.

Siddiqi opened the door and led me in. The video cam was set up on the tripod, but the operator wasn't in the room yet.

Siddiqi leaned over to me and said in a soft voice, "You can call me Smitty. Everyone else does – well everyone on our side." He then whispered, "They're planning an attack soon. It will be handled by an FBI SWAT team. These guys are tough and experienced. Every one of them was a former Navy SEAL. There may be a lot of gunfire. Make sure you and the MacPherson ladies lay low when I give you the word. I'll let you know as soon as it's firmed up. The only thing that can slow it down at this point is snow, which is forecast for the next few days."

The video operator came into the room. I expected him to hand me my script in the normal hilarious English. But apparently the script writer found a new job, maybe spraying graffiti on subway cars.

"You will talk in your own voice," said the producer, who spoke decent English. "I remind you not to say anything out of the ordinary. Just say hello and tell your husband how well you are being treated."

I was ready for my close up and began.

"Hello, Rick. I miss you. Everything is okay here. I am being treated well. It's a beautiful day here in Yemen. I saw on the news that they're expecting an early snow in the New York area. I know how much you hate snow because it slows you down. But I remember that time in Central Park when it was snowing and you and I watched the seals in the pond. We were amazed at how tough the seals were, frolicking in the snow. But cheer up, honey, it will eventually melt and you can go forward with your plans. I still miss my dog Fiddles. He's such a loyal dog, always willing to help me. Well, bye for now, Rick. I'm wide awake after my nap, so I think I'll get some exercise. Love you."

My producer moved his finger across his throat, which I interpreted as a signal to wrap up my broadcast. How apt for him to use a symbol of violence, I thought.

The producer folded up the tripod, hung the camera around his neck and left the room. He yelled something in Arabic to Smitty, who came back into the room to escort me back to my apartment.

"Be careful, Mrs. Bellamy," Smitty whispered.

"You too, Smitty."

I had a feeling that something was going to happen soon. I think Smitty felt the same way.

>

I called Buster and Bennie to my office as soon as I downloaded Ellen's latest video to my iPad.

"I want you guys to see this as I'm seeing it. I didn't want to give it an editorial spin. Here goes."

I propped up my iPad so Buster and Bennie could see it and hit play.

"Hello, Rick. I miss you. Everything is okay here. I am being treated well. It's a beautiful day here in Yemen. I hope it doesn't snow where you are. I know how much you hate snow because it slows you down. But I remember that time in Central Park when it was snowing, and you and I watched the seals in the pond. We were amazed at how tough the seals were, frolicking in the snow. But cheer up, honey, it will eventually melt and you can go forward with your plans. I still miss my dog Fiddles. He's such a loyal dog, always willing to help me. Well, bye for now, Rick. I'm wide awake after my nap, so I think I'll get some exercise. Love you."

Buster looked at me. "That's one tough broad you married, Rick."

"I couldn't agree more," said Bennie.

"Okay, let's dissect this," I said as I wiped sweat off my forehead.

"First thing I noticed is that she talked about snow and how it can slow down plans. She's letting us know that she gets it."

"And her comment about the seals and how tough they were frolicking in the snow," said Buster. "She's telling us that she knows the plan involves SEALs—or former SEALs—and she doesn't give a fuck whether it snows or not."

"And notice that she said she was wide awake after her nap," I said. "That's code from our novel, meaning, 'I'm ready.' And her comment about her imaginary dog Fiddles blew my mind. Remember, Fiddles is an AK-47. She commented that 'Fiddles' is such a loyal dog, always ready to help—*always ready to help.*"

"Rick," said Bennie, "your lovely wife just told us that she's good to go."

CHAPTER FORTY FOUR

At 7 p.m. on December 14, we all met at Colonel Drury's house for what would be our final planning meeting before the raid on the safe house. I sipped milk, about the only substance I seemed able to keep down. I like to think of myself as a tough guy, a guy who can take a hit and hit back harder. I'm a former Marine, combat tested, and I'm an FBI agent with a caseload of rough stuff. Bullshit. I was a fucking wreck. Ellen is the most important person in my life, and she'd soon to be involved in a gun fight. I thought it was time for some leadership and guts, and the person who needed it most was me.

All of us, including Bennie who served as a combat physician with the Army, are former military men. Everyone on the SWAT team are former SEALs. I think Leo, a former SEAL himself, is happy with that. I know Colonel Drury likes it. I noticed that we'd been addressing one another by our former military titles, or present title in the case of Lt. Leo. At first I thought this was kind of dumb, but then I realized it was a way to remind ourselves about what would soon happen – a violent military confrontation, one that required strict discipline.

"Gentlemen," said Lt. Leo, "today is Monday, 12 December. I want to launch the raid on Tuesday of next week, 20 December. The moon phase will give us maximum darkness. But we may have a problem. The weather forecast is for moderate to heavy snow on Tuesday night. If that happens, I'm going to put off the raid."

"But the long-term forecast calls for possible snow almost every day for the next six days," said Colonel Drury. "It's also supposed to be unseasonably cold for the next few weeks. If that stuff starts to pile up, we're looking at a steadily degrading situation. You're the boss of this operation, lieutenant, but I just wanted to share some of my thoughts."

"Colonel, I hear you, and believe me I'm listening. I'm not only listening, I'm open for suggestions. Let's talk about it."

"Here's one way of looking at it," I said, sipping my milk, "if they're suspecting a possible attack, and according to Smitty they're not, they wouldn't expect it under bad weather conditions. Remember Eisenhower agonizing about D-Day. The weather was bad, but he knew that one thing on his side was surprise. Don't you guys have white camouflage uniforms?"

"Yes, we do have white uniforms, specifically for snow operations. As I said, I've checked the moon for December 20 and it will be a new moon, meaning that it will be as dark as possible. When Smitty turns off the lights, we'll have plenty of darkness, except for the snow."

"Another thing to consider," said Buster, "if we go on Tuesday and it does snow, the stuff will be powdery, not caked with ice. If the long-term forecast holds true, the situation will worsen rather than improve for the next few weeks."

I almost felt sorry for the young lieutenant. The guy couldn't be much over 32 years old, and his shoulders carried more weight than they should for a man of his age. But he was the commander of the operation and the decision was his. He walked over to the pot of coffee, obviously trying to buy some time. He filled his cup and came back to the gathering. He set his cup down and put his hands on his hips.

"Okay, it's a go. Next Tuesday at 0230, snow or no snow."

We all stood and applauded, fist pumped the air, and cheered. My stomach wasn't in complete agreement, but I knew that it was the right choice. Lt. Leo smiled and let out a long breath.

The raid would begin soon. And my Ellen would be in the middle of a firefight.

CHAPTER FORTY FIVE

I've got to stop saying to myself that I can't believe this. I really have to stop thinking that I'm a just a peaceful architect and I don't need this crap. It's time to channel some of my husband's courage. A raid is going to happen, and it's going to happen soon.

I also realized that it was time to bring Margo and Jane into the loop. They didn't understand my code, like Smitty, so I had to communicate with them in writing, lest the camera and microphone bugs suspect something.

I walked into the living room of our suite. Margo and Jane were reading and chatting. I held a Scrabble game under my arm that I found in the closet of my room.

"How about a game of Scrabble?" I asked.

"I'd love to, hon, but I'm trying to finish this book," said Margo. "Maybe tomorrow."

I walked over to Margo, bent over and drilled my eyes into hers. I really didn't have any idea how to "drill eyes," but I'd seen Meryl Streep do it in a movie, so I figured I'd try being an actress. It worked. Margo realized, apparently, that it was important to play

Scrabble – *now*. She and Jane stood up and walked over to the card table in the middle of the room.

"This is going to be a different kind of Scrabble game," I said, making it up as I went along. "It's called Cheater's Scrabble," whatever the hell that is, I thought. "Each of us will spy on the person to our left, and pass a written note to the person on our right, saying what we think the next word will be. It's a lot of fun." (Even though I never heard of it before.)

We all drew our tiles.

"Looks like I go first." I didn't draw the high tile, but Margo and Jane were starting to get what I was up to.

I passed the first note to Margo on my right.

"An FBI SWAT team is going to raid this place any day now. Smitty told me that they're all former Navy SEALs. The plan is for us to remain in this room when the shooting starts. Siddiqi is an inside operative and he's on our side. I call him Smitty. He'll alert me and I'll tell you two."

"Oh, I've got a great word," I said, for the benefit of the wall bugs.

"Do we have a weapon of any kind?" Margo wrote, slipping the note to me.

"Yes, I have an assault rifle under my bed. It's called an AK-47, also known as a Kalashnikov. I've been trained how to use it."

"I'm quite familiar with the AK-47, dear. Do you have an extra clip?" wrote Margo.

Wow, I thought. This lady isn't afraid to mix it up.

"Yes, I do," I wrote. "When the raid starts, I'll keep the rifle trained on the door, and I'll blast anybody who walks through, except for Smitty or SWAT team member."

"I have to visit the ladies room," I said, gathering up the notes to flush down the toilet.

When I returned, Margo wrote, in her patrician way of communicating, "And what weapon shall I use? *A Stern Look of Disapproval?*"

"There's a baseball bat over there in the corner," wrote Jane. "I was captain of the women's softball team at Princeton. I can swing a mean bat."

"Stay crouched behind furniture, Jane," I wrote. "A bat isn't much good against bullets."

"I assume the raid will be at night," wrote Margo.

"Yes, it will be in the wee hours of the morning. I suggest that you do like I've been doing, and practice sleeping during the day."

"I must have had too much coffee this morning. I have to pee again," I said, gathering up the notes.

When I returned to the table, Margo wrote, "Is my husband aware of this?"

"I have no idea. All I know is that it's going to happen."

"Is there anything we can do to help," wrote Margo. "We have one gun and one baseball bat among the three of us. Surely we can do something."

"What we have to do," I wrote in all caps, "is follow orders from Smitty or the SWAT team. They know how to pull off something like this. We don't."

"I notice you two have strong bladders," I said. Just me bouncing up and down to visit the ladies could look suspicious, I thought.

"Thanks for reminding me, dear. I think I shall pee," Margo said as she gathered up the latest notes.

We finished the Scrabble game. Jane won, or so I announced to the sensing devices.

"I'm tired," said Margo. "I think I shall retire."

"Hey, it's only midnight," I said. "How about another game?" I gave Margo my newly- discovered Meryl Streep eye drill.

"You're right, Ellen. Late night is a wonderful time for games," said Margo. "I'll keep score."

Although I didn't know it at the time, our game playing would soon come to an abrupt end.

CHAPTER FORTY SIX

I mam Muhammed Bushariff, our new friend Mike, called this morning on a secure line we provided him, and asked to meet me in a small cafe in lower Manhattan. We had agreed that it was a bad idea for him to visit any of us at FBI headquarters. He said he had something urgent to tell me.

I walked into the cafe and looked around for Mike. He wasn't there. Out of the corner of my eye, I saw a man wave to me. The guy was wearing a Yankees cap backwards, along with a Yankees jacket over a jogging suit, and a pair of wraparound sunglasses. Holy shit. It was Mike. This guy would make a good spook, I thought.

"Rick," said Mike in a soft voice, "there's a guy I have to tell you about. I didn't think he was in the United States, but he is. The name is Ali Bashara, but he now goes by the name he was born with, Phillip Murphy. He's one of the homegrown radicals you guys worry about. Not only is he homegrown, but he's in charge of handling all the native terrorists in the country. He's the reason your database is starved for information. From what people have told me, he's with al-Qaeda, but his roots are in ISIS. I last heard about him a few years ago, but now he's surfaced big time."

"What more can you tell me about this guy?"

"Rick, he's a ruthless killer, as bad as they come. Even radical turds that I talk to from time to time are afraid of this guy. From what I've heard, he kills for the thrill of it, not for any religious or ideological reason. He just loves to kill, and he's good at it. His specialty, from what people have told me, is beating and killing women. I heard a story, confirmed by two people, that he once beheaded a woman in front of her family because her hair wasn't covered. This guy is bad. And now he's back here in the States."

"Do you have any idea where this woman-killer is located, Mike?"

"All I know is that he's somewhere in Tenafly, New Jersey."

"Excuse me, Mike. I have to visit the men's room."

I barfed until I thought my body would run out of fluid. A notorious woman murderer is holed up in the same house as my Ellen and the MacPherson women. I splashed cold water on my face and dried it off. I smacked myself a few times to try to get some color back into my face before I returned to our booth.

"Anything else, Mike?"

"Yes, but I have no idea what this is about. I've heard snippets of conversations that Bashara, aka Phillip Murphy, has something to do with a plot involving shopping malls. That's all I can tell you. I'll let you know when I hear more."

As we walked to the door after our meeting, Mike turned to me and said, "Be careful, Rick, and be careful with your family. This scumbag would love to chop off your head."

We shook hands, after which I returned to the bathroom to throw up again.

CHAPTER FORTY SEVEN

"Brother Ali, you wish to see me, sir?" said Smitty.

"Yes, and do not call me brother Ali, or even Ali. My name is Phillip Murphy, and you are to remember that. Do I make myself understood?"

"Yes, br...I mean Phil."

"I have noticed," said Bashara/Murphy, "twice in the past week alone, that two of our women guests have been seen with their heads uncovered by their veils. On one occasion, the Bellamy woman was seen wearing Western clothing, not even covered by her burqa. This must stop immediately. The next report that I hear about this immodesty, a severe beating will be in the offing and I shall personally handle the chore. They're too valuable to kill, but if I deliver a beating, they will wish they were dead. I want this warning to come from you, not me. As one of their handlers, you will be the one to deliver the message. I am serious, Siddiqi, deadly serious."

Margo, Jane, and I had just finished breakfast. We heard a loud pounding on the door. Holy shit, I thought, could this be the raid?

The door swung open and in walked Smitty.

"This is absolutely unacceptable," shouted Smitty, pointing to our uncovered heads. "Your infidel morality, or rather lack of morality, will no longer be tolerated. You must be covered at all times, including your heads, even when you are in this room. I or one of my brothers may walk in at any time, and we refuse to be confronted with your heathen ways."

Obviously, Smitty was doing a command performance for the listening devices, but he seemed like he needed to deliver a strong message. Hell, I thought, better from Smitty than from one of the scumbags.

Without saying anything, the three of us immediately covered our heads.

The raid can't come soon enough, I thought.

⛨ ⛨

"Rick, it's me, Smitty."

"It's Smitty on the secure line," I yelled.

Everyone froze because Smitty's orders were to use the secure line (we hoped it was secure) only in an emergency.

"Things are starting to get dicey here," said Smitty in a hushed voice. "I get the impression that the boss, Bashara, is itching to start beating the women. He's only looking for a pretext. He has a reputation for getting carried away. He's a fucking sadist and he's looking for an opening. I recommend that you guys be prepared to launch the raid on a moment's notice."

Smitty's messages to us were usually quick and to the point. His editorial comments put us all on edge.

"Okay, guys, lock and load," shouted Lieutenant Leo. "Be ready to go on my command."

Thank God it was dark, I thought. At 7 p.m., it was inky black because the moon was obscured by a low cloud cover. It was Thursday, and the raid wasn't supposed to happen until the following Tuesday, but sometimes you don't get to pick your own schedule. There was no snow on the ground and that was a good thing. The only real difference was that the SWAT team would be attacking a houseful of people who were awake. Awake and armed.

Both Bennie and Buster walked over to me.

"I can only imagine what you're going through, Rick." Bennie said. "Just remember, pal, you're not involved in this operation. Let the SWAT team handle it. They're better at it than you. They'll keep Ellen safe."

Buster handed me a glass of milk.

CHAPTER FORTY EIGHT

The MacPhersons and I had just finished dinner, and we agreed to play Cheater's Scrabble later. Jane walked over to the cupboard and reached up high to get a new tin of coffee. As she reached, her upper arms squeezed against the hood of her burqa, causing it to fall to her shoulders, exposing her long blonde hair. The scene was picked up by one of the monitors on the wall.

A sudden pounding on the door scared the hell out of us. A guy who Smitty had told me was the boss man, Bashara himself, walked into the room followed by one of our handlers carrying a pistol. I recognized it as a Colt 45 because Rick has one. Smitty had told me bad things about Bashara. If there was such a thing as a face that said "cruelty," his was that face. He smiled, he actually smiled, while he narrowed his eyes.

"So you have decided to disobey my command and show us your heathen ways," said Bashara as he held a lead pipe, smacking it against the palm of his left hand. "You women are infidel scum, and you are about to learn the way of righteousness."

He walked over to Jane MacPherson and smacked the pipe right across her pretty face. Margo screamed and got out of her seat. The assistant held his gun to her head. Bashara then took a full swing with the pipe across Jane's knees, causing her to fall face down to the floor. He then held the pipe over his head with both hands, and brought it smashing down onto Jane's shoulder blades. He held the pipe over his head again, positioning himself to deliver another crushing blow.

At first I felt numb, then scared, then petrified with fear. But anger started to muscle out those emotions. I was watching a lovely young woman being savagely beaten by a sadistic prick. My mind was consumed by one thought – I'm going to stop this. If my life ends there, so be it. I'm going to stop this bastard. But how?

"Hold on, please," I yelled, holding both hands to my mouth, channeling my inner actress. "I have to throw up."

"Do not delay, infidel bitch, I want you to see this."

I ran into my room, reached under my bed and picked up the AK-47. I made sure that the gun was in firing mode, placed it into a fold of my burqa, and slipped the extra clip into my bra. I walked back into the room. Rick's training on assault rifles came back to me – shoot the man with the gun first.

I raised my AK-47 from underneath my burqa, pointed and fired a short burst at the gunman, as Rick had trained me. I then fired at Bashara, who held the lead pipe over his head, poised to strike Jane again. He fell to the floor. Margo reached down and took the assistant's pistol and expertly pulled back on the slide, racking a bullet into the chamber. Holding the gun barrel pointed up like a trained cop, she ran to Jane and stroked her hair.

"Be still, honey. Ellen and I can handle these scumbags."

Bashara groaned. I knew I hit him with at least four rounds, so it must just have been his lungs expelling his last breath. Margo walked slowly over to him, leveled the gun, and blasted half of his head across the floor. A Colt 45 is like a small cannon, I remembered Rick telling me.

"I didn't want the poor dear to suffer, Ellen," she said.

Funny how you remember things at the oddest times. I recalled seeing a photo of Margo MacPherson on the cover of *Vanity Fair* next to an article titled "The Most Elegant Woman in America."

⊷ ⊶

"Bring it on, bring it on, bring it on!" we heard Smitty yelling into his radio from down the hall.

We heard running footsteps. "Is that you, Smitty?" I screamed.

"Yes, I'm coming into the room."

Smitty walked in, his rifle held down. He looked at Bashara's body next to the assistant.

"Holy shit," said Smitty. "I'm glad you ladies are on my side."

He held up his finger to his lips and said, "Quiet!"

He looked up at the ceiling. We could hear footsteps.

"I've got footsteps above me, section A3," Smitty said to his radio. Section A3? Wow, these guys had really prepared, I thought.

"They're friendlies," shouted Lt. Leo into his radio. "Hold your fire, Smitty."

Smitty shushed us again. "Our job right now is to listen."

We heard two bursts of gunfire upstairs, followed by thuds. I prayed that the thuds weren't SWAT team agents. We then heard footsteps running down the hall. Smitty jumped into the hallway, dropped to a knee and opened fire. We heard a thud.

"Sections A3, A4, A5, and A8 are secure," we heard somebody yell over the radio. "Smitty, Give me a count from your position."

"Two down in A3, and another in the hall," said Smitty with military precision and calmness.

"Okay, I've got a total of eight, which means there's one more to go," yelled Leo.

We heard a burst of gunfire outside toward the front of the house. Leo looked out at the driveway and saw the man lying on the ground with an agent standing over him.

"Make that zero, the number we've been looking for," shouted Burton. "All the enemy are dead. *Operation Betsy* is a success, thanks to Smitty and my SWAT team."

"And thanks to a couple of tough women in section A3," said Smitty. "I need medical assistance in A3." he yelled into his radio.

Bennie Weinberg came running into the room. As a psychiatrist, he was also trained in internal medicine. I knew Bennie had an army background as a combat physician., and it was obvious that he was accustomed to trauma scenes as he approached the beaten and broken Jane MacPherson.

He dictated into his recorder as medics entered the room to take Jane to the hospital.

"I see a fractured clavicle and scapula on the left side, two orbital fractures to the face and a nasal fracture. Knees look bad, possible patellar fractures to both. Edema at all fracture sites. I'm going to poke you a bit, honey. It may hurt. Just tell me what you feel."

Bennie poked, pressed, and prodded Jane MacPherson and finally announced to us and his dictating machine, "The good news is that there are no apparent internal injuries, just the orthopedic ones I mentioned."

Bennie stood as the medics lifted Jane onto a hospital gurney.

"What happened to *them*?" asked Bennie, pointing to the bodies.

"Let's just say their women beating days are over," said Margo as she put the gun on a table.

Bennie took out his dictating machine again and said, "This is Dr. Weinberg with an addendum. The scumbag who did this is dead. End of report."

We heard loud footsteps coming quickly down the hallway.

"Oh shit," said Smitty, "did we miscount?"

He held up his rifle and stepped into the hallway. "Freeze!" we heard him scream.

"My name is Rick Bellamy. You must be Smitty."

Smitty walked back into the room, smiled and said, "Mrs. Bellamy, there's a gentleman here to see you." It was Rick. Oh my God, it was Rick.

"Have I mentioned how much I love you?" I said as I wrapped my arms around his neck.

"Not since your last video."

"Just hold me," I said. "I just want to feel you against me. I thought I'd never see you again."

I nestled my face into his chest and started crying. Hey, I'd held it in long enough – time to let my emotions be honest with themselves. I really thought I was going to die while in captivity. Holding Rick was almost surreal.

We continued to hug, forgetting that we were in a room with about ten other people and a couple of dead bodies.

Margo MacPherson walked over to us. She extended her hand to Rick.

"Hi, I'm Margo MacPherson. You two should get a room."

I laughed and said, "Soon enough, Margo."

Angus MacPherson walked in. Rick told me that he alerted Angus as soon as the raid started. He actually broke down crying, something I couldn't imagine from Angus.

"Margo, it's been many long months. You look more beautiful than ever, except for that thing," he said, pointing to her burqa. "I just saw Jane being wheeled to the ambulance. I told her we'd see her at the hospital. My helicopter will take her to Columbia Presbyterian. The chief of orthopedics is a good friend of mine."

He then turned to me.

"Lassie, you saved the lives of my girls. Jane told me all about it as they were putting her into the helicopter. You're more than I ever expected from an architect. By the way, are you willing to go forward with the plans for the shopping malls – the plans you've wanted all along?"

"I've got the rough drafts done, and I can finish the finals in no time."

"Oh, I should mention to you, lass. I'm giving you a wee bit of a bonus – five years' worth of the estimated losses you're saving me with your plans. That comes out to be about $18 million. And I'll make it clear to your partners that the bonus is for you, not for the firm."

I gave Angus a hug, then looked at Rick and said, "That should cover a few bills."

Sometimes I say the lamest things when I'm feeling emotional.

⊷⊶

The scene of the recent violence was quickly turning into a party, thanks to the booze wheeled in by Colonel Mark Drury, the next-door neighbor and hero who Rick had just introduced to me.

"Your husband is one hell of a guy. I've had a first-hand view of the stress he's been going through, knowing that you were only a couple of hundred feet away. This man really loves you."

I started to feel weepy again, but I just gave Colonel Drury a hug.

"I hope you have an appetite because I just called a terrific caterer," said Drury.

"If falafel is on the menu, Colonel, I will shoot you."

"Buster," I yelled as my favorite spook walked into the room, "you can take the worried look off your face now."

"Worrying is a spook specialty," he said as he gave me a hug.

"Hey, Rick," said Buster, "how about a glass of milk."

"Actually, I think I'll have a Scotch on the rocks."

At my suggestion, we all moved into the sunken den, the largest room in the house. Call me old fashioned, but I just don't like partying around dead bodies.

⊷ ⊶

FBI Director Sarah Watson entered the house. She immediately walked over to Rick and me and gave each of us a hug.

"As you know, Rick, our country is facing an ongoing crisis. President Reynolds calls it World War III. But I want you two to take a vacation. With the horror you've both been through in the past few weeks, I don't want you to burn out. We'll have a quick debriefing at Federal Plaza tomorrow and then I want you guys out of here. So find someplace nice. Relax, read romance novels, and just be with each other. Your country owes you some time off."

Just before midnight, Rick and I said goodbye to our fellow partiers. We took a cab to our apartment. We had some catching up to do.

CHAPTER FORTY NINE

When Ellen and I got back to our apartment, we walked in the door, and Ellen put her arms around my neck.

"Now where were we?" she said.

We each took a shower and met in the living room. Ellen, God bless her, was wearing nothing but one of my men's white shirts, which always drove me crazy – and that was where we left off before she was kidnapped. She sat on my lap. I blew a breath on her neck, which she loves.

"The thought of never seeing you again almost killed me," I said. "The past few days tore me up. Lean over, let me smell your skin. The night you were taken from me is a memory I need to get rid of. It was like the life was squeezed out of me. You know how much of a control freak I am. Not knowing where you were and not knowing how to find you was an experience I want to banish from my brain."

Ellen rested her head on my shoulder.

"Hey, tough lady, you were the real hero tonight."

"If some jerk hadn't left that AK-47 out in the open, Jane may be dead. I have no doubt that Bashara, that sadistic bastard, would have started on me and Margo as soon as he was done with Jane. I never shot anyone before. Hell, I never even aimed at someone. But killing those two bastards doesn't bother me a bit."

"That's you, Ellen. You care about people, and you put your life on the line for Jane MacPherson. The guy with the gun could have popped you as soon as you walked into the room."

"Rick, if you saw what Bashara was doing to that poor girl you wouldn't say that. He made it impossible for me *not* to do something. I had to help her."

She nuzzled her nose behind my ear and kissed me on the neck. I didn't want it to end. I wanted the feeling to linger as long as possible.

Exhaustion overcame us. Although we both expected an evening of love-making, we both nodded off as we sat on the couch. I picked Ellen up, carried her to the bedroom, and rested her on the bed. As I climbed in next to her, she mumbled, "Abuvouoney." I think she wanted to say, "I love you, honey." She fell fast asleep, and within moments, so did I.

⤜⬩ ⬩⤛

"*Stand down, motherfucker!*" Ellen screamed as she sat bolt upright.

"Easy, babe," I said as I pulled her close to me. "It's just a bad dream, I'm here with you." She fell back asleep.

"*Margo, duck!*" Ellen yelled a few minutes later, holding my hand and pointing it at the wall as if it were a gun. She was sitting up again. I held her again as she sobbed. Ellen was sweating like a pitcher of ice water on a hot summer day. I got up to get a towel to dry her off.

We both slept fitfully through the night. I thought Sarah Watson's idea of our going on vacation was a good one.

CHAPTER FIFTY

O ur debriefing with FBI Director Watson began at 11 a.m. I knew I had to be alert because this was an important meeting, but I had little sleep. Okay, time to focus, I thought to myself.

"I'm going to say something that I'm sure Director Carlini of the CIA would say, or President Reynolds himself would say for that matter. Last night was another battle of World War III, a successful battle, thanks to a platoon of brave FBI SWAT team people, thanks to the careful planning by Rick and Buster here, and also thanks in no small part to Rick's courageous wife, Ellen. Rick, you married well."

"I couldn't agree more, Madam Director."

"But this was only *one* battle," Watson said. "The enemy wants to kill us, and to do it constantly. A new phrase has crept into our vocabulary, 'TV Fear.' When we wake up in the morning, most of us click on the television to catch the weather and the morning news. Now we're afraid to hear about the latest terror incident. Make no doubt about it, folks, al-Qaeda, ISIS, and the legions of lone wolf terrorists are starting to have an impact on American society. People are afraid to commute, afraid to walk into their buildings, afraid to take a cruise. And if it weren't for the operation last night, al-Qaeda would have pulled off a spectacular event next year, an event that would have made people afraid to go to a shopping mall. It isn't my purpose today to sprinkle cold water on the well-deserved celebration last night – and it was a hell of a good party. Rather it's my purpose to keep us thinking about things that we don't know about, things that haven't happened yet. With people like Rick from the FBI and Buster from the CIA, we have great leaders in this war effort, and we need more. We need ears to the rails, boots on the ground, eyes open. Both Buster and Rick are working on exactly that."

She poured herself a glass of water. This lady gives a hell of a speech, I thought. She said all of the right things and said them with authority. I was proud to work for her.

Watson cleared her throat and continued.

"But for two weeks we're going to do without the services of our own Rick Bellamy. What he and his wife went through in the past few weeks makes us all cringe. Two people who thought they'd never see each other again. Rick will be on two weeks leave and please don't text or email him without passing it by me or New York FBI Director Auletta. I want these two to relax."

So I was about to take a vacation. Two weeks of spending time with the woman I love, the woman who I thought was going to be killed. Two weeks of not worrying about the world unraveling. Two weeks of not checking email and text messages constantly. Two weeks of bullshitting myself that I actually know how to relax.

But I can do it.

I think.

CHAPTER FIFTY ONE

"Christmas in Aruba. This is really going to happen, Rick. We're going to enjoy each other and not worry about anything. We're going to relax and recharge. We're gonna chill."

"Rick?"

"What?"

"Have you been listening to anything I said?"

"Sure, everything."

"I'm not going to quiz you because I know you weren't listening. Hey, hon, we're about to catch a flight and I can see that you're doing nothing but connecting dots in your head. You're looking for more patterns when you should be thinking about relaxing."

I put my arms around her and kissed her. Ellen was right. I was still at work, even though we were waiting for the doorman to come and pick up our suitcases. We were about to fly to a beautiful spot, and all I'm doing is working in my head.

"Okay," I said, "I promise. I'm going to unwind with the love of my life, and I'm not going to sweat my case files. We're going to swim, scuba dive, read books, and make love."

"I'm going to keep you to that promise, Rick. We're about to fly to a beautiful waterfront house in Aruba and it's ours for two weeks – alone. Gimme a kiss, handsome, to seal the promise."

I grabbed for the remote.

"While we're waiting, let's just check the Weather Channel."

"Fuck the weather, Rick. I don't want to hear some TV reporter say 'We have breaking news…' So what if it's raining in Aruba? We can think of plenty of things to do indoors. I know I can."

The doorbell rang and the doorman came in to pick up our luggage. Ellen looked at me with her eyebrows raised as if to say, "Don't forget your promise."

⟞⟝ ⟞⟝

We'd been in Aruba for just a couple of days, and Rick was keeping his promise. I thought he was actually starting to relax. It isn't just that he's a workaholic or an obsessive compulsive. Rick is a dedicated man. He loves his country and considers it his personal responsibility to make things right. He's a professional, one of the things I love about him. I enjoy the fact that I admire the guy I love. But I'm going to keep him to his promise.

We spent the morning snorkeling in the beautiful blue green waters off Aruba. The temperature was high, around ninety-five, and the sun was blazing. We lay down on a recliner under an overhanging roof. A gentle breeze swept away the humidity. I spotted a little iguana climbing up the post. Ever since I was a kid, I liked lizards. Not a girlie thing, I know, but I thought they were interesting. I nudged Rick and pointed to the iguana.

"You like those things?" asked Rick.

"Why not? They're friendly, industrious, and kind of cute. Like you."

"Great, my wife thinks I'm like a friggin lizard."

He leaned over and kissed me.

I dozed off for a few minutes, more relaxed than I could remember. When I awakened, Rick was propped up on an elbow, staring at me. I stroked his face.

"And you were about to say?"

"I was just thinking. You've won a lot of architectural awards. I bet you could walk off with a gold medal for best looking architect in a bikini."

"Thanks, baby, but I don't think there's a competition for that prize."

"We should go inside," Rick said. "I don't want you to get sunburned."

"Rick, we're in the shade. We're under a roof."

"Well, I think we should go inside anyway."

"Why?" I asked, but I was pretty sure I knew why.

"We should rinse off the salt water. A nice warm, soapy, sudsy shower should do the trick."

"And what will we do after the shower?"

"Let's go inside and I'll show you."

"Rick, there's something we haven't talked about at all. We haven't discussed my big bonus from Angus MacPherson. $18 friggin million dollars! And we haven't even talked about it."

Rick got up from his chair and moved it next to me. He put his arm around me and kissed me on the cheek.

"I've never thought a hell of a lot about money, Ellen. I get a reasonable salary from the FBI, and your huge design fees got us a three-bedroom apartment in Manhattan. I heard MacPherson say it, but I haven't thought about it since. I don't want to sound like a soap opera, hon, but having you alive is all I've been thinking about recently."

"But $18 mil is a nice piece of change, Rick. We could even retire."

"And then what would we do? We're too young to retire, and you're too serious a woman to become idle rich. You love your work, and I love my work, and that's a good thing."

"Maybe we could set up a foundation to help kids or something?"

"Now you're talking. You're talking like my Ellen."

We were enjoying an early lunch on the patio of our vacation house. After we finished, we got up to bring the dishes inside. As we walked through the door, Rick put his finger over his lips to give me a "shush" signal and grabbed my arm. He put his dish down on a small table and gently pushed me behind a concrete wall at the entrance.

He tiptoed to a closet, reached in and took out his gun. He chambered a round and held it in both hands pointing down.

"Come out and put your hands where I can see them!" Rick yelled as he raised the gun.

The cleaning woman dropped a basket of laundry, put up her hands, and started crying.

"Oh, shit," said Rick. "I'm sorry. Here let me help you with that stuff."

I walked in, gave the woman a hug, and said in Spanish, "My husband is a very nervous man. He's sorry. Everything is okay."

She wiped her eyes, gave a short laugh and said, "Si, Señora."

I looked at Rick.

"You know, we're not supposed to be here, Rick. We blew it. The schedule calls for the house to be cleaned between eleven and noon on Tuesdays and Thursdays."

"I feel like a jerk. I'm sorry, babe."

"Are you sure you don't want to talk about retirement?"

"No, I enjoy scaring the shit out of cleaning ladies."

CHAPTER FIFTY TWO

"Bennie, it's Buster. Please come to my office."
I missed having Rick around to swap ideas. He's the best FBI guy I've ever worked with, and he's also a good friend. I agreed with Director Watson sending Rick and Ellen on a vacation, not that it's my place to agree or not. After the horror the two of them went through with Ellen's kidnapping, they needed some time off. Big time.

"Hi, Buster, what's up?" said Bennie as he walked into my office.

"Ben, I want to sort some things out with you. I need the input of a psychiatrist."

"Anxiety?"

"No, it's not about me. Shit, my life is one big anxiety attack. I just live with it. I want to talk to you about our new friend, Imam Mike. This guy is like a gift from heaven. He's singlehandedly populating our database with names that we never had. He even warned Rick about that sadistic scumbag Bashara. Thank God Ellen shot the bastard, but the point is that Imam Mike had him fingered."

"So what are you concerned about, Buster?"

"Mike seems to think he's a born-again spook. Since he flipped his head away from the side of darkness, he thinks he's part of our team."

"Well isn't he?"

"Yes, but the guy has me worried. I didn't wake up one morning to discover that I was a spy, a CIA operative, a spook. I've had years of training and it's still going on. Mike is a religious cleric and he doesn't know the first thing about clandestine ops. I need your input Bennie. What makes this guy tick? If I can figure that out, I may be able to handle him better and keep him from getting his head chopped off."

"His personality profile, Buster, is that of a helper. In one way or another, we all want to please superiors, not just for career moves, but for the sense of satisfaction we get from making 'the boss' happy. He sees you and Rick as his superiors. It's obvious when I watch him. He's now on the inside, and he's taking a lot of pride in it. He wants to help."

"But will his desire to help get him into trouble? Will he take risks that could expose him? I don't want to lose this guy, Bennie. He's the most valuable mole we've got, probably the best we ever had."

"Talk straight with the guy, Buster. The next time you meet him, remind him how dangerous spying can be. Remind him that he can't risk being tagged as a man who asks too many questions. Also remind him to keep up appearances as an imam. The next time a terror attack happens, remind Mike that he can't go off on a rant from the pulpit. That's how that imam in Michigan got whacked. If I were you, I'd meet with him as soon as you can."

"On another subject, Bennie, do you think al-Qaeda's found a replacement for Bashara?"

"Yes, Buster, my guess is that they've already found a new head man. And here's what worries me – they're going to be looking for some payback. We shot down the biggest terror plot to date with the MacPherson shopping mall plan. Make no mistake about it: the scumbags will be looking for blood – soon."

CHAPTER FIFTY THREE

"Aadil Ammar, may peace be with you,"

"Are you a fool, Joseph Portman? You are never to use my Muslim name, and you are not to say 'peace be with you.' My name is Dennis Borman. You dishonor our slain leader Bashara, I mean Phil Murphy. He has given you the new rules, Joseph, and we must all use extreme caution. Understood?"

"Yes, Dennis."

"I assume you have heard the details about the infidel raid on our house in New Jersey?"

"I have, Dennis. It was in all the newspapers. I wept when I read that brother Bashara, sorry I mean Murphy, was killed."

"In that one raid, our gigantic plan for next year was dashed. I can tell you about it now because it is no longer a plan. We were to destroy five large shopping centers across the country at one time. Because of a radical design of the buildings, we estimated that we could have killed 75,000. But that is now over."

"Does that mean things will get quiet for a while?"

"Of course not, Joseph. We always have more plans."

"But the most important thing I have to tell you is this. The CIA had an inside man at our New Jersey house. It is the only logical explanation for what happened. That's why you have to be diligent about only using your infidel name. You are also to avoid radical websites. I know you've been told all this before, but it's now critical. It's essential that we 'fly beneath their radar,' as the infidels like to say. You will now take orders from me. I have overall command of our plans for the next year. And I have some interesting assignments for you, Joseph."

"Praise Allah, Dennis, I hope to hear of them soon."

"And, Joseph?"

"Yes, Dennis?"

"Please no talk about praising Allah. We will praise him by our actions."

CHAPTER FIFTY FOUR

"Good morning ladies and gentlemen, Shepard Smith for Fox News. I have a horrible report to start this Monday morning. A commuter train derailed as it entered Union Station in Chicago. Preliminary reports indicate that the derailment came immediately after a large explosion in the locomotive. We don't have reports on casualties as yet, but because it happened at the height of rush hour, the fear is that the toll will be high. First responders are on the scene, and we've received reports that Union Station is in absolute chaos."

⇌ ⇋

Rick and I began our Monday after our vacation listening to Shepard Smith on Fox News report the commuter train disaster in Chicago.

That evening we met back at our apartment after a hellish day. It had only been two weeks since our wonderful vacation in Aruba, and now it was back to the shit. It was an unusually early hour of 6 p.m. for the two of us to be home, but we both felt the need to steal some quiet time together. We arrived at the same time. As soon as we walked in we hugged, our usual procedure.

"You look like hell, honey. I'll make us a couple of martinis."

"I suppose I shouldn't take this crap personally, Ellen, but it isn't easy. A voice in my head is screaming at me, asking me what I could have done to prevent this. And I'm not coming up with any answers."

"Rick, you're one of the best FBI agents in the country. I've heard Director Watson say that herself. You're brilliant, you're a patriot, but you're not omniscient. You can't control everything that goes on in this insane world. Nobody can. Shit like today is the new normal, and we all have to get used to it."

"But I thought we had it figured out. We had the data, we had the plan, and we had the people to execute it. Everything looked perfect. Now, I don't know what we've got."

I held Rick's face in both hands and kissed him, a long lingering kiss. He looked so upset. I was obsessed with making his pain go away. In our relationship, when he's in pain, I'm in pain. And I don't like to be in pain.

"Well I know what you and I have," I said. "Us. Whatever crap they fling our way, I have Rick and Rick has Ellen. That, honey, is a constant of the universe, and don't forget it."

"My God," said Rick, "you have a beautiful way with words. Yeah, there's you and me, and that's the most important thing in the world."

"So why the frown on your face, hon?" I asked. "Do I have to drag you back to Aruba?"

"I feel like I live my life waiting for another shoe to drop," said Rick.

"Well, drop both shoes, take a nice shower, and let's relax," I said. "I have a surprise for you."

Angus and Margo MacPherson had become our good friends. No doubt this had a lot to do with Ellen saving the lives of Margo and Jane. Angus had virtually adopted Ellen as a second daughter. It was no surprise when Ellen handed me an envelope with MacPherson on the return address.

"Rick, isn't this sweet?"

Two tickets to the Super Bowl were in the envelope, courtesy of Angus.

"I've always wanted to go to a Super Bowl, Rick. We can afford the tickets, God knows, but the only ones we ever had a shot at were lousy seats. Look at the great spots that Angus gave us, two of the best seats in the house."

"It takes somebody like Angus MacPherson to pull that off, hon," I said. "The game is on February 1, a week from now. Hey, maybe we can take a couple of extra days and enjoy some time off in beautiful Arizona. It may not be Aruba, but we agreed we'd try to grab short vacations."

"You don't have to convince me, honey," Ellen said.

CHAPTER FIFTY FIVE

"Hey, wake up, sleepy head," said Ellen. "We have to catch a flight to Arizona at noon."

It was Saturday, January 31, the day before the Super Bowl.

I got out of bed, stretched, and looked out the window.

"Hey, where the hell did Manhattan go?"

Ellen walked next to me at the window. What we saw was beautiful. The city was pure white, covered in a few feet of snow, swirling in funnels driven by the wind. We couldn't make out the cars parked across the street, just snowy mounds.

I clicked on the TV, something I hate to do first thing in the morning.

"A beautiful snow-covered good morning, folks," said the TV weatherman. "It may be beautiful, but it's also serious. That weather front we've been tracking for the past few days shifted to the Northeast, and is bringing the New York Metropolitan area its worst blizzard in at least 10 years. The snow's been falling steadily at about two inches an hour and shows no signs of letting up. It's a slow moving storm and our forecast is for a whopping seven feet across the Tristate region. All area airports, including JFK, LaGuardia, MacArthur, and Newark are closed with no incoming or outgoing flights expected until late tomorrow. So stoke up the oven, put on some chicken wings, and enjoy tomorrow's Super Bowl from the comfort of your own living room. The weather in Glendale, Arizona, is expected to be perfect for game time tomorrow."

I was pissed, although it's kind of stupid to be pissed off at a snowstorm. Things happen, don't we know.

"Damn," Ellen shouted. "I was so looking forward to going to the game. Getting Super Bowl tickets with good seats is like winning a lottery. Maybe Angus can wangle a couple of tickets for next year. I don't even have any greasy comfort food for tomorrow. We can't even have a Super Bowl party."

"Maybe they'll shovel the sidewalk by tomorrow so I can go to the deli down the block and get us some wings." I was trying to be helpful. We were both totally disappointed.

I got back into bed and Ellen climbed in next to me. We watched the reports of the storm.

"Well, at least we have a wide screen TV," I said, trying to be positive.

⇒⊩ ⊩⇒

What my life would be like without Ellen is a thought I don't want to contemplate. I was forced into exactly that thought when she was kidnapped a few weeks ago, but she's here, very much here, the best part of my strange life.

We spent the snowy Saturday playing a Scrabble tournament. After six games, we were tied at three games each. Earlier, we each worked out in the small gym that occupied one of the bedrooms in our apartment. When you have a wife who earns a ton of money it makes for some conveniences. The bonus that Angus McPherson gave Ellen would make for a few more. We were stuck in our apartment, but, typical of Ellen, it was fun. After our work-out and Scrabble tournament, we decided to watch old movies that we had saved on the DVR, something we always intended to do but never found the time.

On Sunday, it continued to snow without letting up. After a leisurely breakfast, we read *The New York Times* on our Kindles be-cause the paper delivery couldn't make it through the blizzard. I was absorbed in the Sports Section, reading everything about the big game. I took out a calculator, and began computing my own odds.

"Connecting dots, honey?" Ellen asked.

"Can't help myself, babe. I'll be ready to take a bet from you shortly."

"As soon as you see a pattern?"

"There's always a pattern. Always"

CHAPTER FIFTY SIX

We invited a new couple from upstairs to join us for the Super Bowl. Phil and Marilyn Beaton recently retired from Apple and decided to return to New York City where they grew up.

I'm not a heavy eater, and neither is my slender Ellen, but something about Super Bowl says, "Eat." Fortunately, the deli down the block was open after the snow was shoveled, and I bought a few bags of wonderful caloric fatty stuff.

Game time was 3 p.m., Mountain Time, or 5 p.m. for us. Phil and Marilyn came down at two and we played a game of Scrabble waiting for the game to start.

"So you folks were supposed to be there," said Phil. "Bad luck, but we're happy you wanted to share the day with us. Marilyn has an old saying, and I'm beginning to think it's true over the years – everything happens for a reason."

We played a second game of Scrabble before the game. Phil and Marilyn are 49ers fans, and Ellen and I like either the Giants or the Jets. None of those teams was in the Super Bowl so our interest in the actual game was somewhat casual. At 4:30 I clicked on the

TV. I hate all the repetitious blabbing that goes on before a game, but I figured we'd check out the last minute pregame chatter.

"Although the record snowfall in the Northeast has stopped some fans from coming, it appears that most made their plans early based on the weather forecast, and we have an almost full capacity crowd of 63,400 at the University of Arizona Stadium here in Glendale."

"Most Northerners made their plans early," I said. "That's what we should have done."

"Hey, Ellen, where would our seats have been?" The TV was showing views of different sections of the stadium.

Ellen got up and walked over to the television.

"Right there," said Ellen, pointing to the TV, "under the control booth on the fifty-yard line. Great seats, but hey, we have a good view from here."

The phone rang. It was Imam Mike.

"Rick, where are you?"

"Stuck in New York, Mike. We were supposed to be at the Super Bowl, but our flight was cancelled. What's up, Mike."

"This morning I heard all kinds of chatter about a bomb going off over the heads of the 'infidel Bellamys.' Something about a roof falling onto your seats. Stay put, my friend. I'll call you if I hear anything else."

I didn't want to spoil the day, so I didn't announce what Imam Mike had just told me. What the hell could it be? I thought. We watched the coin toss for the kickoff. It was heads, and the New England Patriots chose to receive. The Seattle Seahawks will kick off into a slight wind.

We heard a loud rasp and the screen went blank.

"Damn," I said, "there must be an electric outage."

"But the lights are still on," Ellen said.

Ellen clicked to another channel. An ashen-faced reporter was babbling on about something as he clenched his ear bud with his right hand.

"There's been an explosion at the Super Bowl," he said, holding his earpiece. "We have little to go on at this point, but it seems that the control booth at mid-field has exploded and fallen to the seats below."

Ellen walked over to the couch and sat next to me. We looked into each other's eyes, remembering that just a few weeks ago we thought we'd never see each other again. She pressed her face next to mine and said in a choking voice, "The control booth fell on top of the section where we were supposed to be sitting. Rick, we're alive."

I switched the remote back to NBC, the network that was broadcasting the game. The scene was from the NBC studio in New York. From what we'd just heard, we were sure the broadcasters on site in Arizona were dead.

"Information is just coming in now," said Sam Powell, a new anchorman for the network. The poor guy was choking back sobs, the kind of sobs you hear from somebody who just lost a bunch of friends.

"We have a report, which we haven't yet verified, that a small private jet slammed into the control booth just minutes ago. According to a person on the scene, the plane must have carried a large bomb because the explosion was so great. The plane hit the booth dead center, destroying it and causing the remnants to collapse onto the seats below."

Ellen and I looked at each other as he said that – the seats below – *our* seats.

The camera view panned out, apparently taken from the Goodyear Blimp over the stadium.

"Oh Dear God," said Powell, doing his best to control his emotions. "From the air it appears that a large part of the stadium has been destroyed. That had to be one gigantic bomb. We're not going for any close ups folks. The view is likely to be pretty gruesome."

My cell phone rang. It was Buster. I had called him the day before to let him know we weren't going to the game.

"Holy shit, Rick. It was those two homegrown scumbags that we traced to the flying school in Phoenix, Tony Lombardo and George Rendell. I just got confirmation from the owner that they flew a jet from the adjacent airport this afternoon. Imam Mike from Brooklyn tipped me off. We had them, but they got us first. Oh, and they also had some help from inside the stadium. It looks like there were a bunch of dumpsters filled with explosives behind the control booth."

I told Buster about the phone call I had just gotten from Mike.

I was too numb to think about security clearances and "need to know," so after I got off the phone I simply announced to Ellen and our friends what Buster had just told me. I also told them what Imam Mike told me.

"Wasn't Muhammad Atta on a watch list of suspects before 9/11?" asked Phil Beaton.

"Yes," I said. "What these people are doing is turning our society inside out. Pretty soon people are going to start to clamor for locking people up first and asking question later. We knew who these guys were. We had them on our radar."

The tension in our apartment was almost painful. I was happy that our friends from upstairs were with us.

"President Reynolds said it recently, folks," said anchorman Sam Powell. "World

War III has begun, and we've just witnessed another battle, a battle like all of the ones we've seen since the attacks of 10/15, a battle that we weren't prepared for."

When he said that I just put my face in my hands.

"Hey, Rick," said Phil Beaton, trying to be helpful. "You just told us that you had those guys in your crosshairs. Don't blame yourself. All you can do is continue to look for clues and try to head off trouble when you can. You can't just go in with guns blazing and kill suspects. That's not what this country's all about. Hey, let's look at the one positive thing this afternoon. You and Ellen are alive."

I walked over to the window. The snow was still falling and the streetlights below created a beautiful scene as the sun began to set, a peaceful scene. Peace? That's a word I love, a word that we seldom hear. Ellen walked up next to me and put her arm around my waist. Phil and Marilyn correctly judged that we needed a couple of minutes alone. Ellen looked up into my eyes.

"When will this end, Rick?"

"End? I don't think that's part of the pattern."

CHARACTERS –
THE SHADOWS OF TERROR

Akhbar, Gamal – see Atkins, Charles
Aldonzo, Giuseppe - Commercial jet captain
Aadil Ammar - al Qaeda leader, aka Dennis Borman
Atkins, Charles – CIA Agent, aka Buster
Auletta, Barbara – Director of New York City FBI Office
Beaton, Marilyn and Phil – The Bellamy's upstairs neighbors
Bellamy, Ellen – Architect and Rick Bellamy's wife
Bellamy, Rick – FBI Agent
Bukdama, Ali – al Qaeda operative, aka Bob Margano
Bashara, Ali – Radical leader, aka Phillip Murphy
Bushariff, Muhammed – Muslim cleric, aka Mike
Buster – CIA Agent
Carlini, William – Director, CIA
Cummings, Randolph – Secretary of Defense
Drury, Mark – Retired Marine Colonel
Farooq, Ahmed – Al-Qaeda operative
Fleming, Nigel – Interpol agent
Hannon, Nancy – FBI Agent
Lopez, Phil – FBI Agent
Magda – Angus MacPherson's assistant

MacPherson, Angus – Real Estate Developer
MacPherson, Jane – Angus MacPherson's daughter
MacPherson, Margo – Angus MacPherson's wife
Margano, Bob – al-Qaeda operative, aka Ali Bukdama
Martin, Zeke – FBI Agent and Rick's partner
McGrath, Carmella – Mayor of Tucson, Arizona
McClaren, Denise – Suspected terrorist
Margano, Bob – Executive at MacPherson Security
Muktada, Abbas – American jihadi, aka Joseph Portman
Palmara, Frank – FBI agent
Portman, Joseph – American Jihadi, aka Abbas Muktada
Siddiqi, Baqir – aka Smitty, CIA Agent
Simonetti, Mike – Harbor pilot in training
Turner, Mike – FBI Agent
Watson, Sarah – Director, FBI
Weinberg, Benjamin – Psychiatrist and detective, NYPD

ABOUT THE AUTHOR

I'm the author of *The Gray Ship* (Coddington Press 2013), book one of *The Time Magnet* series. It's a story of time travel, romance, and a nuclear warship that finds itself in the Civil War. *The Thanksgiving Gang* is the sequel, *A Time of Fear* is Book Three in the series. *The Skies of Time,* is Book Four in the series.

This book, *The Shadows of Terror* is the first book in The Patterns Series.

I have also published five nonfiction books: *Justice in America: How it Works—How it Fails.* (Coddington Press, 2011); *The APT Principle — The Business Plan That You Carry in Your Head.* (Coddington Press, 2012); *Boating Basics, the Boattalk Book of Boating Tips(* Coddington Press, 2013)*; How to Create More Time* (Coddington Press, 2014). I'm a lawyer and a veteran of the United States Navy. I live in Long Island, New York with my wife Lynda.

Please make sure you don't miss out on my forthcoming books.

Visit my website, www.morancom.com and click on the "subscribe and get updates button."

I hope you enjoyed *The Shadows of Terror.* If you did, please consider leaving a review on amazon.com.

The Scent of Revenge **is the next book in The Patterns Series.**

The world is at war – World War III.

FBI Agent Rick Bellamy and his wife, Ellen, are in the middle of a sinister terror plot.

Someone is attacking young prominent women, inflicting a horrible disease.

Nobody knows its origin, nobody knows how to stop it, nobody knows how to cure it.

Rick Bellamy and a team of scientists want to go on offense. But how?

Will the lives of the women be changed forever? When will the attacks stop?

Coming in July 2015.

www.ingramcontent.com/pod-product-compliance
Lightning Source LLC
Chambersburg PA
CBHW070110260626
47160CB00004B/1401